It was time to call it quits. Cody had had nothing but grief since coming to Turtle Rock. He'd been performing his own version of the Sun Dance, torturing himself to prove he was worthy to be part of his dad's family. And for what? So his grandfather could take some sneaky, white kid's side.

Acknowledgements

Family support is crucial in every project and I am most indebted to my husband Carmen, to our son John and son-in-law Ron for their individual creative efforts. Our daughters, Johanna and Cara, came through with doses of encouragement when it was most needed. Special thanks to my young nephew, Adam, for reading the manuscript and offering his invaluable perspective.

My writer friends are many and they were available with their time, support and useful suggestions for this project. Virginia Smiley proved a sensitive and dependable sounding board. Mary Jane Auch and Herm Auch were generous with their expert input and help. I am grateful to them all.

Sun Dance at Turtle Rock

Patricia Costa Viglucci

Stone Pine Books
Patri Publications
Rochester, New York

Sun Dance at Turtle Rock is an original novel published by
Stone Pine Books, an imprint of Patri Publications. This book
is available at special quantity discounts for fund raising or
educational use. Please address all inquiries to Stone Pine Books,
Patri Publications, Box 25184 Rochester, NY 14625.

Viglucci, Patricia Costa
Sun Dance at Turtle Rock

Summary: Cody, a bi-racial 12-year-old, visits his estranged white
grandfather in the Allegheny foothills of Pennsylvania and finds both
acceptance and prejudice against a backdrop of adventure.

ISBN 0-9645914-9-9

Library of Congress number 95-69286

First printing, January 1996

Cover illustration-Ronald L. Bartlett
Layout and Design -- JayVee Graphics

All the world is filled with His glory!
Isaiah 6:3

Chapter 1

The small air terminal on top of the mountain was empty except for the ticket agent. Good. Cody Spain wasn't in any particular hurry to meet his grandfather.

He glanced toward the counter, and the agent, peering over reading glasses perched low on his nose, pointed to Cody's bags.

"These what you're looking for?" He motioned to the blue gym bag and large gray suitcase lying to one side.

"Yes, thanks."

"Plane must have been near empty?" Cody nodded and went over to pick up his luggage. He'd been the only one to get off, the rest of the passengers going on to Pittsburgh.

"Somebody meeting you?" The agent bent over his newspaper, revealing a large bald spot on top of his head.

"My grandfather. Or maybe my aunt." Cody hoped it would be Aunt Charlotte. He could barely remember either of them, but his aunt was the one who had begged his mother to let him visit. His mother liked and trusted Aunt Charlotte.

A loud buzzing sound caught Cody's attention and he tried not to smile as a large, persistent fly blitzed the bald spot.

"You headed for Bradford?" The agent yawned, swatting furiously to no effect.

"Turtle Rock."

The agent shook his head as if Cody had made a poor choice. He yawned again. "Small place. Takes longer to spit than drive through town." He swatted again, missed. "Waiting section's over there." He pointed to the four metal chairs against the far wall and winked at Cody. "A bit crowded tonight, but you should be able to find a seat."

"Thanks." Cody swung the gym bag up with one hand and grasping the handle of the much heavier suitcase with the other slid it along the floor. At 12, he was small for his age. If only he'd start to grow some, show signs of taking after his dad.

He was halfway to the chairs when the door from the parking lot opened and slammed shut. Footsteps echoed loudly in the high-raftered room and a quiver went through Cody.

"Zachariah Spain?" The words were so soft, Cody barely heard them. He turned and looked up into fierce blue eyes under bushy white eyebrows.

"I'm Zachariah Spain," he answered. "But I like to be called Cody."

His grandfather snorted. "Calling you by your middle name was your mother's doing. Vanessa claimed two people answering to Zack was enough for any family."

Cody peered up at the large figure in the clean blue overalls and work shirt, glimpsed the pale scalp under the faded red hair.

Even though he thought he knew what to expect, the flesh and blood Zachariah was a surprise. He hadn't thought his grandfather would be so...so...pinky white.

"No problems on the plane?" Zachariah's voice was flat. "Those small commuter jobs are all that land here anymore."

"It was fine."

"This all of your luggage? Not much for a whole summer."

"I might not be staying that long..." Cody stooped to pick up the gym bag.

Zachariah got to it at the same time, his large, sunburned, freckled hand swallowing up Cody's dark one before loosening its grasp.

Cody glanced up and saw the bored ticket agent studying them, trying to figure out how they fit together as if they were a puzzle.

Maybe they were: white grandfather, brown grandson. In the middle of another yawn, the agent met Cody's gaze, but only for a second.

"*Arragh*!" Cody fought down a laugh as the agent gagged and sputtered. The fly, a Stealth ace, had found a new target. Talk about spit.

"Let's go." Zachariah who had missed the excitement, lifted the heavy suitcase easily with no sign of the heart problems that Aunt Charlotte had used to get Cody's mother to change her mind.

Without bothering to see if Cody was following, Zachariah strode out to the unpaved parking lot to a dusty gray Blazer.

Cody felt small and unimportant trailing behind. He glared at Zachariah's unfriendly back.

There had been no polite questions about Cody's mother or his stepfather Pell. But that was understand-

3

able. His grandfather wouldn't want to hear about the black man who had taken his dead white son's place. Or about the new baby coming in the fall.

Lucky kid. He or she wouldn't have to live in an in-between world.

Zachariah opened the tailgate and put the gray suitcase in the rear and waited until Cody tossed in the gym bag, then slammed it shut. They got in and the Blazer started down the mountain.

"Your Aunt Charlotte and your cousins would have come, but her husband's mother is sick. They all went to Warren. Be getting back late. You'll have to make do with me tonight."

The small knot that had formed in Cody's chest when he stepped off the plane grew larger.

From the high front seat, he watched as a chipmunk scurried in front of them and disappeared into the thick underbrush. The sun had set and the road, in shadows, snaked down and around the mountain, cutting through the deep Pennsylvania woods.

"Are there bears in there?" The words came out unexpectedly.

"Could be." Zachariah's voice was hard with anger as if Cody had asked some awful question like why did his mother and his grandfather hate each other so much.

Cody shifted in his seat and looked out the window, his throat suddenly full, his eyes stinging.

Zachariah didn't want him there. Didn't want a brown grandson crammed down his throat.

He stole a look at him. His grandfather looked healthy enough--and tough. Like he'd never cared what anybody thought about him.

A little moan escaped from deep in his throat causing Zachariah to look his way. "No need to bawl."

"I'm not!"

"You didn't want to come." When Cody didn't answer, Zachariah persisted. "Well, did you?"

"No!" he lied. Half lied. He'd wanted to come and he hadn't.

"I didn't think so." Zachariah sounded pleased as if he'd proved a point. "So why did you?"

Cody looked out the window. He didn't know the answer.

His grandfather cleared his throat. "I'm none too happy myself about the situation. Charlotte had no business going behind my back begging your mother to let you come. Vanessa made herself clear plenty of times how she felt about your daddy's white family."

The knot threatened to push through Cody's rib cage. He tried to take a deep breath and failed. They rode in silence to the outskirts of the town, the hillsides dotted with an occasional farm.

The Allegheny mountains were all around them, steep and forbidding. He felt closed in. His mother said his father, Zack Jr., had loved the hills and deep woods.

Well, Cody wasn't his father. Wasn't his grandfather, either. He scanned the dark green of the mountain forests. You could almost imagine there were Indians in them, especially now that the sun had gone down. He closed his eyes for a minute and saw a brave, bow in hand, move silently from tree to tree.

When he opened them, they were in town. The street was lined with large old houses with wrap-around porches, bay windows and the little towers he thought were called turrets.

He blinked once and they were in the middle of the business section: A couple of stores, two banks, a filling station and diner. The only people around this time of night were some guys getting in and out of their pickups. Their faded jeans and tee shirts made him feel over-

5

dressed in his new khakis and polo shirt.

The stores ended and the houses began again. The agent was right. There wasn't much to the town. No wonder buses and trains didn't go to Turtle Rock.

"Dumb name, Turtle Rock."

"What?"

Cody slid down in his seat. He hadn't realized he'd spoken out loud. But it was a dumb name. Pennsylvania was full of them. Peach Bottom, Bird-in-Hand, Intercourse. Jelly Belly hadn't believed his eyes when Cody had pointed out the last one on the map. And a little ways back he'd seen a sign for Cyclone.

The Blazer made a right turn, then crossed a small bridge. A pond was on their right. They were headed up another hill and he realized the town was built on two mountain sides facing each other.

"That's Turtle Rock Lake." Zachariah motioned toward the water. "You fish?"

"No." It made Cody want to laugh, calling this puddle a lake.

At the topmost street, the Blazer turned left. There were only a few houses on the winding road with fields of wildflowers and weeds in between. Some kids were walking towards them on Cody's side, all with hair the color of the buttercups. When the Blazer passed them, a girl about his age turned around to stare. She probably thought Zachariah had trucked in a fresh air kid for the summer.

No, Turtle Rock was small enough everyone had to know Zack Jr. had gone to Rochester and married his assistant, a black woman.

Everybody knew that Zachariah had raised a stink about the marriage. But it hadn't done him any good, so he'd patched things up with his son before the car accident that had taken Zack Jr.'s life

6

Afterwards Zachariah had asked--no, ordered--Cody's mother to come to Turtle Rock so he could take care of both of them. That had been six years ago and the last time Cody had seen any of his father's family.

As the Blazer slowed, Cody drew in his breath. This was where his father had grown up. The old farmhouse perched on a slope, a small sag visible in the newly shingled roof. As they turned, he spotted a gray barn, a small pond and a whole forest of Christmas trees marching up the mountain behind it.

A man on an extension ladder was giving the farmhouse a fresh coat of pale yellow paint. Cody focused on the man's white blond hair, lighter yet than the paint.

"Nels Larsen," Zachariah explained as he gave a wave. "He's lending a hand with the sprucing up."

Oh?" Cody took stock of what he'd seen. "How many people in this town anyway?"

Zachariah, half out of the Blazer, turned back, a frown on his face. "Less than 2,000. Mostly Swedes. Why?"

"Just wondered."

"You going to sit there all day?" Zachariah pulled open the tailgate and lifted Cody's bags out.

Slowly, Cody climbed down from the Blazer and went around to get his belongings. He knew now that his mother wanted no part of Turtle Rock not just because of the way Zachariah felt about black people. It was clear she and Cody would have stood out like sore thumbs. And in six years nothing had changed.

Now, unless he was mistaken, he, Zachariah Cody Spain III, was the only non-white person in the whole town.

Chapter 2

"Wipe your feet," Zachariah said at the back door. "Max gets hot under the collar if we track in mud."

"Is it his house?"

"Max is a she. Carries on like it was hers, squawking if things aren't to her liking. Helps out by coming and hoeing through the place every so often. Charlotte's idea."

Cody followed his grandfather into the kitchen. An old, beat-up rocker stood next to some big windows through which he could see the pond and the evergreens on the darkening hillside.

A pie cooling on the round, wooden table filled the room with the scent of apples and cinnamon and started his stomach growling. He'd been too nervous to eat before getting on the plane and no snacks had been served on the short flight.

"Come on. I'll show you your room. Up the back stairs. You can see the rest of the place later." Zachariah picked up the suitcase easily and opened the door to the stairs.

A window at the top was open, billowing curtains trapping the pine-filled breeze. Cody followed his grandfather down the wide hall. "This one's mine. Spare room next. You're in here."

Two double beds, dressers and night stands filled the big room. Cody put his bag on the bed nearest the two windows which overlooked a side yard. "Whose room was this?"

Zachariah stared at him from under bushy eyebrows. "Your aunt's a long time ago. Why?"

"Just wondered."

"Bathroom's across the hall. Come down when you get squared away and you can have a bite to eat."

Cody waited until Zachariah was downstairs before searching out the bathroom. His face in the old mirror had a pinched look. He looked around some more before going down, noting again the room with the closed door at the far end of the hall.

Was it his dad's room?

He was about to go find out when he heard Zachariah calling from the foot of the stairs. He delayed at the top until the apple and cinnamon smell floated up to meet him. Zachariah had cut and dished him up a large slab of pie and motioned for Cody to sit at the round table.

"Here's a glass of milk to wash it down. Eat up." Cody picked up the fork, put the napkin in his lap.

He took a bite of warm pie. "It's really good."

"The apples are from my Mutsu trees, a cross between a Japanese apple and Golden Delicious. My best crop yet last year. Gave some to Max. She makes up the pies and puts them in her deep freeze. Bakes one when the notion strikes her. Guess I'd better have a piece myself." Zachariah was almost sociable talking apples.

Cody made short work of the pie, refusing a second

piece.

"If it's all right, I think I'd better phone my mother. She said to call collect."

Zachariah's mouth got that tight look. "I can afford a phone call, I guess. In there, in the living room."

Cody found the phone between a pinkish brown couch and a matching easy chair. The overhead light was dim and that and the faded furniture made him homesick. Over a fireplace there was a framed Bible verse and in a corner a grandfather clock had stopped at 2:30.

He dialed direct and his mother answered on the first ring.

Her voice was high and thin, the way it got when she was worried. "How was the trip? It started storming here after your plane took off. Some lightning."

"No problem, no rain or anything," he soothed. "It only took a half hour. I sat next to a man who was going to Pittsburgh and we talked."

"Was your Aunt Charlotte at the airport?"

"She's away, but she's coming back tonight."

"Zachariah met you?"

He made his voice light. "Uh, huh."

His mother sighed. He never could fool her. They talked some more, she made him promise to write and after Pell said hello and to keep his chin up, he put the phone down.

He didn't feel like going back in the kitchen just yet so he looked around some more.

He read the hand-stitched Bible verse. "Love One Another" had little lambs embroidered around it. One lamb--the littlest one--was black. It had its heels up and looked like it was dancing, its tail wagging. Cody grinned and wished he could remember Grandma Gemma. She'd died a couple of years ago. Vanessa had had a bad case of the flu and she and Cody had not attended the funeral.

More cause for bad blood between Zachariah and his mother, he guessed.

"So you know how to smile." Zachariah had come into the room and Cody turned around. The blue eyes and bushy eyebrows were fiercer than ever. Cody thought his grandfather had a lot of nerve talking about smiles. He hadn't let one slip yet.

"You about ready for bed? It's going on 10:30." Zachariah glanced at a small clock on top of the TV cabinet.

Cody wasn't, but he didn't want to make a big deal out of it. Maybe he'd read in his room. He'd packed some comics, a computer game and a book on Indian rituals Pell had bought for him on a recent visit to the museum.

He said goodnight, trying to ignore the sinking feeling as he went up the stairs. Nights were always worse when you were in a strange place, especially in a place where you weren't wanted.

He turned the pages of the book, unable to concentrate, then switched off the light. He closed his eyes, trying to think of something pleasant. Jasmine Allen floated into view. They'd been on friendly terms when school had ended. Her family went to the Baptist church too. Trouble was Monroe Martin, a year ahead of them, had also started noticing her. She'd probably have forgotten Cody by the time summer was over.

The next thing he knew the sun was shining in his face. He dressed quickly, dragged the covers up on his bed and went into the bathroom to splash water on his face.

There was no one in the kitchen, but Cody could hear noises. It sounded as if Zachariah was in the basement. He went to open the door to call down when a screen door slammed somewhere else in the house and someone came racing through the front hall."

"Grandpa! Grandpa! Where are you?"

It sounded like trouble. Zachariah obviously heard it and thought so too. He came tearing up the stairs. For an old man who was supposed to have heart problems he could move fast.

It was the girl, Jemma, the cousin who was a year or so younger than Cody. She was out of breath. "Grandpa, come quick. Timmy fell down the outdoor steps to the basement. His head is bleeding and Mom can't stop it."

"I'm coming. You got any ice at your house?"

"Not much."

Zachariah looked at Cody. "You and Jemma get some ice out of the freezer. Follow me over." And he was gone.

They stared at each other. Curiosity replaced the worry in her dark brown eyes. A few freckles stood out on her flushed face as she pushed back wisps of shiny brown hair.

"I'm Jem."

"I know."

"You're not anywhere near as dark as I thought you'd..." She broke off, flustered. "I mean..."

"We'd better hurry." Cody opened the door. He found two trays of ice behind some white freezer packages. Jem held open a plastic bag she pulled from one of the cupboard drawers and he emptied the trays in it. "Let's go."

She led the way, tearing out through the front hall and door, kitty-cornered across the road to the gray house with blue shutters. Timmy could be heard before they hit the yard.

Jem bounded up the steps to a wrap-around porch and went back to the kitchen door. Zachariah was sitting down with Timmy on his lap, pressing a wet wash cloth to the back of his head.

"Good, here's the ice brigade," Zachariah said. "Let's have a couple of cubes wrapped in this cloth." His voice was calm and comforting, not at all like when he talked to Cody.

Cody's Aunt Charlotte was wringing her hands. She gave Cody a quick smile when she saw him, then grabbed the cloth, put some of the ice in it and handed it to Zachariah.

"The bleeding's not stopping, Dad. I never saw a tiny cut spurt like that before."

"Puncture wound. Most have fallen on some of the gravel he threw in the stairwell. It'll stop. Doesn't look too bad. We just have to get him quieted down."

Timmy continued to wail. When the ice was put on the cut, he yelled even louder and his mother let out a little moan.

"Let's try the puppies," Zachariah said after a minute. "Jem, you two go get a couple and bring them up here."

"Come on, Cody," Jem said. "They're down in the basement." He followed her down the stairs.

"Dad's making this into a playroom for us. The pups are over here in the laundry room. We put up the gate so they can't get out."

The pups were making little mewling noises. Mandy, the mother, came to Jem to be petted and Cody drew in his breath. The pups were beautiful. Jem picked up a little black one and handed it to him and took a brown one for herself. He took it carefully, laughing when the puppy began to lick his hand.

"What kind are they?"

"Mutts," said Jem. Mandy's part Lab, the father a setter.

Cody cradled the puppy and it licked his chin. His heart cannonballed. The pup was the sweetest thing he'd ever seen.

Timmy had stopped yelling. Now he was sobbing, great big sobs causing his chest to go in and out.

"Timmy, look what we've got. It's Spats, your favorite." Jem held her puppy up and a little pink tongue licked Timmy's face. He continued to sob and pointed at Cody.

"Want other one, too." Cody took a step forward and let the black pup lick Timmy's hand.

"What's doggy's name?" Timmy asked between sobs. He looked at Cody. Cody glanced at Jem who shook her head. "This is J.B." Cody said quickly, "after my best friend, Jelly Belly."

"Jelly Belly," Timmy repeated. He smiled. Giggles replaced the sobs.

Aunt Charlotte started laughing. "God, Dad, why aren't I gray? This boy is going to be the death of me."

Zachariah took the ice away to check the bleeding. The spurting had stopped. He looked at his daughter and his lips twitched.

"You plant red potatoes, you get red potatoes," Zachariah said.

Jem grinned at Cody's puzzled look. "Mom was a heller. Grandpa tells us stories all the time about how she was always getting in trouble when she was little. See that mark at the top of her nose? She went down Grandpa's front steps on a sled when she was four."

Cody look at his aunt. It was hard to think of her as a heller.

"Timmy takes after Mom. Only he's ten times worse. I take after Daddy. Quieter."

Timmy wiggled down off Zachariah's lap and started chasing J.B. around the kitchen. For the first time Aunt Charlotte seemed to really see Cody.

A grown-up version of Jem, she swept a strand of hair out of her face and exclaimed, "Poor Cody, what an awful welcome. I'm your Aunt Charlotte." When Cody didn't say anything, she said, "I'm your father's sister." She looked down into Cody's face and her smile got a little funny as if she might cry, but she didn't.

"Green eyes just like your daddy's. And look at those long lashes! Mouth like his too. You stubborn?" She grinned at him and he grinned back forgetting to be embarrassed by all the comments.

"Sometimes."

"Uh-huh, I thought so." Her arms went around him and he felt a shudder go through her.

"Oh, babe, do you know how long it's been since we've seen you? You weren't much bigger than Timmy, the last time your Daddy brought you home..."

She broke off and dropped a quick kiss on his head. "It's so good to have you here."

It was the kind of greeting Cody had hoped for, one that made last night's welcome only a bad dream. He felt right about being there, but it lasted only a minute.

"He didn't want to come!" Zachariah boomed, his words making Cody's face burn. "Fine kettle of fish you've stirred up, Charlotte."

Chapter 3

Aunt Charlotte turned to Cody, a pleading look in her eyes. "You'll at least give us a try, won't you?"

He nodded, angry with his grandfather for embarrassing him.

"Now tell me about your mother. How's Van feeling? The baby's due the end of summer isn't it?" Aunt Charlotte's voice was a warm blanket chasing away the chill produced by Zachariah's words.

He nodded again because he couldn't be heard over all the noise. Timmy, on hands and knees, was growling at the puppies.

"Timothy Leone, stop teaching those pups bad habits," Aunt Charlotte scolded. She looked at Cody. "Did you have breakfast? When I called earlier, Grandpa said you were still sleeping."

"Not yet."

"What kind of cereal do you like?"

"Any kind."

Zachariah stood up. "Well if the excitement's over, I've got to get back to the house and see if Nels needs some help."

He knelt on the floor and turned Timmy so he could see the wound. "Too small for stitches. Wash it again and put on some antiseptic. Call Doc if it'll make you feel better, Charlotte."

"I will. You're not going to go up on the ladder are you, Dad? To help Nels paint, I mean."

Zachariah snorted. "I plan on staying on the ground. I'll paint the back door. Then I'm going to the barn to make some sawdust."

Jem grinned at Cody. "That's Grandpa's little joke. It means he's going to his workshop. Right now he's making a beautiful porch swing for Mom's birth..." She broke off, covering her mouth with her hand.

Zachariah shook his head and gave Jem a stern look, but there was a twinkle in the blue eyes, his voice soft.

"Should have known better than to let you in on a secret, Jemma. You're your grandma all over again. Couldn't keep a secret if her life depended on it."

Cody listened in surprise. So his grandfather could be kind and loving.

Zachariah got up, turning to Cody, his voice full of gravel again. "Do what your aunt says. Make yourself useful." The screen door slammed behind him.

Cody felt his face get warm. He looked up to find Aunt Charlotte and Jem watching, embarrassed looks on their faces.

Cody turned his head and pretended to watch Timmy playing with the pups. He hoped no stupid tears would come to his eyes. A terrible wave of homesickness hit him.

"How about that cereal now?" Aunt Charlotte smiled

at him. "Or I've got a better idea. Some French toast. Jem and Timmy will probably keep you company. Okay?"

"Okay."

"Good, let's get things underway. Cody, will you and Tim take B.J. downstairs, see that he's settled all right? Jem, you take Spats and then come set the table."

In a short time she called them to take their places. Timmy insisted on sitting next to Cody. Standing on the chair seat, he reached for a container of syrup centered on the table.

"Timothy! You're going to fall," shrieked Aunt Charlotte as he began to topple over. Quickly, Cody fastened an arm around Timmy's waist. The chair went over with a loud racket.

Timmy looked at the chair. "Dammit," he said and smiled angelically at Cody. Cody tried hard not to laugh.

"Timothy!" screeched his mother once again.

Jem, too, was trying not to laugh. "Timmy heard Daddy cuss last night when Timmy rode his tricycle into the floor lamp and knocked it over while Daddy was taking a snooze. The lamp just missed Dad's head."

"That's it for you, buster," Aunt Charlotte said. "If you don't take a rest, neither of us is long for this world."

She started to pluck Timmy from Cody's lap where he had landed. But Timmy threw his arms around Cody's neck and refused to let go. "Stay with Cody."

"I give up," Aunt Charlotte muttered. Quickly she forked a piece of toast onto the youngster's plate, poured syrup on it and cut it. Timmy scrambled back to his chair and began eating.

The French toast was good and Cody ate several pieces. Timmy sang quietly to himself as he poked the food into his mouth, using his fingers instead of the fork. Cody smiled down at him and Timmy beamed his angelic smile back, raising a sticky finger to Cody's cheek.

18

"You're getting Cody's face dirty," Jem objected. "He won't want to be your cousin if you do that."

"Cousin," crooned Timmy, trying out the word. He looked at Cody for a long moment, then at the French toast. He stuck out a finger as if to wipe Cody's face, then frowned.

"Cody's face dirty." He looked at Cody's hands and arms. "Dirty all over. Need bath!"

"Timothy!!" Cody heard Aunt Charlotte suck in her breath behind him.

"It's okay," Cody said quickly.

"No, it's not." Aunt Charlotte's voice was strained. "Cody's skin is brown, Timmy. Beautiful brown. Not dirty."

"Dirty, dirty, beau-ful dirty," yelled the little boy, beating on the table with his fork.

"I've had all I can take this morning!" Aunt Charlotte, cheeks red, scooped Timmy out of his chair. He screeched in protest as she carried him toward the stairs.

They could hear him all the way up: "Cody not dirty. Cody...beau-ful brown."

Cody glanced at Jem. He laughed stiffly and she did too, her face flushed.

"You mustn't mind Timmy. He watches TV and sees all kinds of people. But he never seemed to notice the difference."

Cody tried to think of something to say, but there didn't seem to be anything. He couldn't be mad. Not at Timmy. It was the kind of thing you had to expect in a back-woods place.

"Welcome to Turtle Rock," he mumbled under his breath. Jem heard him.

"You don't like it here, do you? But you haven't even seen the town. Have you?"

He'd seen--and heard--about as much as he wanted

to. "We drove through last night."

"That's nothing. I'm going to show you the best part of Turtle Rock. Wait, I'll go tell Mom." She was back in a moment. "Let's go. Mom said to let Grandpa know."

As they crossed the road, Jem pointed out a sign cut in the shape of an evergreen tree with the message, Spain's Tree Farm.

"That's what Grandpa used to do, grow Christmas trees. There are still acres of them up on the hill. Every year we go up and cut one."

Cody traced the feathered edges of the tree. "Grandpa made the sign, too," Jem said. "Wait until you see his shop. He's got a big table saw, a jigsaw for fancy work and a lathe. Sometimes he lets me use them."

"I didn't know girls liked to do stuff like that."

"Why not? It's as fun for girls as it is for guys."

They passed the pond with its small dock on the way to the barn. Cody stopped to take a look. "Can you swim in it?"

"Later in the summer when it gets really hot. It's fed by springs and right now it's like ice."

Cody dangled his hand in the water. Jem was right. Now, the end of June, the pond was freezing cold.

Jem pointed to a spot up on the mountain. "You can see the deer lick from here. Grandpa puts up a salt block to keep the deer from eating his apples, but they still do. It's a good place to think." He ran to catch up with her as she disappeared in a door at one end of the barn.

Inside he got a surprise. He had expected it to be dark, but wide windows had been cut on the back wall looking out on the hill of evergreens. At the far end was the shop and above it a loft.

"Someday Grandpa is going to move in here. As soon as he can get it fixed up. The house is too big for him. He's going to give it to us to live in."

So his grandfather was going to give the house away. So what if it was perfect? It was nothing to Cody.

A machine roared into action. At the far end of the barn, Zachariah was ripping a length of lumber, the scent of freshly cut wood filling the air. He finished and turned off the saw. As Jem explained their plans to Zachariah, Cody looked around. He could see why his grandfather would want to live here. There was room to spread out and it was all open and peaceful with nothing but the trees and mountain to look at.

Zachariah looked over at him, but all he said was, "Don't be all day, you two, and don't do anything foolish up by the lake. It's 15 feet or more in some spots."

"We won't," Jem yelled over her shoulder and started out the door, running down the slope to the road. Cody caught up with her there.

"Don't you ever walk?"

"Not if I can run. Let's start with the lake and the park and you can see the swinging bridge. And then if you want, we can stop at the diner or get an ice cream cone or..."

"My money's still in my suitcase."

"That's okay. I have some from baby sitting Tim. Let's go," and she took off. Cody ran to catch up. Her legs weren't any longer than his but she could really move.

On the side street that led down to the lake, he slowed down to look at an orange nylon tent in front of one of the houses.

"Come on," Jem yelled. "We got one of those at home. We can put it up and sleep out if you want to. Amy Johnson and I started to last summer. About midnight Amy thought she heard a bear and got scared and we had to go in and go to bed. I would have stayed by myself, but Mom wouldn't let me."

"You wouldn't have! A girl--outside alone in the dark."

"I would too! Our windows were all open and Mom and Dad's bedroom was right above us. They'd have heard me if I needed help."

"So why didn't she let you?"

"Because she's a nervous Nellie. I'm not going to be like that when I grow up. I'm going to let my kids do whatever they want to--except really dangerous things."

"Like what?"

"Walking the Kinzua trestle. It's more than 300 feet high. Mom did when she was a kid, before the holes were repaired, but she never told Grandpa and Grandma."

"Maybe your kids won't tell you what they do either," Cody said. "That noise you heard when you were sleeping out? It couldn't have been a bear? Right?"

"Sure it could. People are always spotting bears around here. Just ask Grandpa."

Jem suddenly sprinted ahead to the entrance to the park which sloped down from the road. "Well, say something," she ordered.

"It's okay," Cody said. Jem looked insulted. Water falls near the small bridge they'd driven over last night, were offset by miniature islands at the other end. A swinging footbridge connected the main area to the largest of the islands where a shelter and picnic tables huddled under the pines.

They crossed the narrow footbridge which swayed under their movement. Jem bounded off the footway to the island.

"Welcome to Turtle Rock," she said, and jumped up on a large round, layered rock. "It's how the town got its name."

"It looks more like a hamburger than a turtle," he teased.

"It does not! See down here, this part looks like a turtle's head."

"There's an Indian legend about a turtle holding up the earth," Cody told her. "The Indians had to be the first to see this."

Jem nodded. "They were all around here. Still are. This whole area is called the Seneca Highlands. The Allegheny Reservation is nearby. Cornplanter was another, but the government flooded it, even moved graves, to build Kinzua Dam."

"How do you know all that?"

"Mom and Dad talk about it when we go there. Indians got burned--again." She made a face. "It's kind of a park now--around the dam. You can fish, launch a boat."

Jem was quiet for a moment. "If you want to, we can go over to the courthouse next. There's a museum in the basement with lots of arrowheads and other Indian stuff that was found around here."

"Let's go!"

"Oh, blast it!" Jem stopped, made a face. "Look!"

Cody turned. A skinny kid, about Cody's age, was coming across the swinging bridge."

"It's that nerd Tucker Hubbard." Jem made a gagging sound. "He comes every summer from downstate to visit his grandmother. Mrs. Hubbard lives near us and she likes Grandpa."

"What's his problem?"

"He's big trouble. Watch out for him!"

Chapter 4

Cody could see right off that Tucker Hubbard was a smart ass. He walked across the swinging bridge as if he were king of the roost. Strutting and smirking, he bounced on to the island, battle written all over him.

"Who's your boyfriend, Jemma?" Tucker asked. "He's real tanned for so early in the summer, isn't he?"

"He's not my boyfriend. He's my cousin and he's visiting Grandpa. Not that it's any of your business, Tucker Hubbard."

"Maybe I should make it my business. Where I come from the people with uh--tans--stick to their own neighborhoods." Tucker smirked, clearly pleased with himself.

Cody eyeballed him. "Maybe you should go back there, then."

Tucker was taller than Cody, but he looked like he'd blow away in a windstorm.

Tucker's smirk changed to a scowl. Cody thrust his hands in his pockets and scowled back hoping Tucker couldn't tell his heart was pumping a mile a minute.

"Black people ain't welcome in this town so..."

"Tucker! Tuck-ER!" On the other side of the bridge a big, heavy-set man was bellowing.

"Your dad's calling you," Jem said.

Tucker looked around. "I've got to go now." He glared at Cody. "You have to go past my grandmother's house to get to old Zack's place. I'd run fast if I were you."

"TUCK-ER!!" Tucker's father was starting over the bridge. Without another word, Tucker turned and fled. The man caught sight of Cody and stared, his face hard. When Tucker stopped in front of him, he cuffed him along side the head. Tucker shrieked and started running for the upper road, the man half running after him. "I told you he was a jerk," Jem said in a low voice. "A whole family of jerks."

"Yeah." Cody smiled, but his heart was still pounding. "Let's go look at the arrowheads."

The museum in the basement of the McKean County Courthouse was just up the hill on the other side of the park.

"Jelly Belly would like it here with everything close by. He doesn't like to walk much," Cody told Jem as they headed for Main Street.

"That's the friend you named the pup after? Is he fat?"

"He's skinnier than me. When he was little all he'd eat were jelly sandwiches. His real name is Isaiah, but nobody calls him that."

"What do the teachers call you?"

"Cody."

"You don't like your first name?"

"I like it. Cody just fits me better."

"Zachariah fits Grandpa. It's from the Bible. And Spain

25

is an Irish name. Isn't that weird?"

"Umm." Cody kicked a pebble in his path, his thoughts on Tucker.

"Cody was Great-Grandma's maiden name. Mom says way back we're related to Buffalo Bill."

"Maybe."

"Don't you care about that stuff?" Without waiting for him to answer, Jem went on. "I do. I'm named after Grandma Gemma, but Mom changed the spelling. She says our names remind us where we came from and where we're going."

"Where we're going?"

"What we're going to do with our lives. She says how many belly-dancers do you know named Charlotte or Jemma?"

"None."

"See!"

Cody grinned. "Because I don't know *any* belly dancers!" Jem wrinkled her nose at him and started racing ahead again.

The museum turned out to be just one small room. Cody got a chance to tell Jem some things she didn't know about Indian crafts. There were a lot of arrowheads displayed that had been found around Turtle Rock which got him all steamed up about finding one.

"We should look on land that hasn't been built on," he said.

Jem's eyes lit up. "I know where. Devil's Den!"

"What's that?"

"A bunch of huge rocks, some as big as that gas station across the street. It's on top the mountain behind Grandpa's house. I'll bet the Indians used to take shelter in the caves. Takes about an hour to walk up."

"Can we go now?"

Jem shook her head. "Mom wants me to watch Timmy

for her later. When we go, it'll take the whole afternoon."

"Tomorrow then?"

"Soon," she promised. "Do you want to get something to drink?'

"I'd rather go play with the pups."

"Grandpa doesn't like dogs or we'd give you one. We have to find homes for all but one of them in a couple of weeks. Mom says two dogs are enough. You can come over and play with them all you want to."

"Let's go then."

"As they walked down Main Street, Jem spoke to the few people they passed. A few looked at Cody curiously, but most just smiled.

"You know everybody in town?"

"Almost."

"Weird. In the city I don't even know the people in the next apartment building."

Zachariah was at the kitchen table bent over the sewing machine when Cody walked in.

"See if you can thread this," he ordered. "I can't see the hole even with my glasses." Cody did it on the first try, producing a growl that might have been a thank you.

"What are you sewing?" Something blue lay on the table with a wide strip of blue and white-striped material nearby.

"This nightshirt hits me at the knee. Found some pillow ticking in your grandma's sewing bag and I'm adding a piece to make it longer," he said in a prickly way, as if daring Cody to laugh at him. "Where's Jemma?"

"She went home. We want to play with the pups for a while if it's all right."

"It is. Afterward I want some help from the two of you."

"Okay."

"See that pile of wood next to the barn--under the can-

27

vas. Thought we could stack it on the back porch so I can get to it easier."

"Sure. I can do it by myself. Right now if you want."

"Hold on. No big hurry." Zachariah looked up from the sewing machine. "We didn't get much of a chance to talk this morning what with Jemma running in here screaming about Timothy's accident. Sit down over there." He pointed to the rocker.

Cody obeyed, wondering what was coming next. He rocked carefully and looked up at the mountain to see if he could spot the deer lick then turned back to watch his grandfather.

He didn't know there were people who actually wore nightshirts. Zachariah was from the dark ages in more ways than one.

His grandfather lay the ticking on top of the blue material, lowered the presser foot and sewed a few stitches. Apparently satisfied that it was going to work, he switched the machine off and concentrated on Cody. "You hungry?"

Cody shook his head. "Aunt Charlotte made French toast."

"This is your home for the summer," Zachariah began. "When you get hungry between meals, help yourself. Two rules: You clean up after yourself and don't go snacking so close to meal times you spoil your appetite. I don't much like cooking and I don't want to go to the trouble of fixing something and then have you turn up your nose. Understand?"

"Yes. I like to cook. I can help with that, too."

"You can, can you?" The bushy eyebrows went up. "What's your specialty--TV dinners?"

"I can make scrambled eggs and hamburger and chili."

"Chili, huh? Not too hot, I hope. I know you people like hot foods..."

Cody scowled. "This isn't. Just ground beef and beans and canned tomatoes and onions. I use dry onions, the instant kind. Peeling the regular ones make my eyes burn."

Zachariah snorted. "Nothing like fresh vegetables."

"I made cake, too," Cody said. "Out of a box. For my mother's birthday." Too late he realized he'd said the wrong thing as Zachariah's eyes started darting fire. It wasn't going to be easy. Zachariah could say whatever he wanted, but Cody would have to watch his tongue.

"How are your school grades?"

"Okay. Mostly As and Bs."

"You plan on going to college?"

"Yes. The checks--the ones you send every month-- they go in the bank in a special account."

Zachariah's mouth got that tight look. The money his grandfather sent was another sore point. Cody's mother would never use it for any of their expenses or spend any on herself--even before Pell had come into the picture.

The front screen door banged. Jem skidded to a stop in the kitchen.

"The doctor says Timmy doesn't have to have any stitches. We just have to keep him quiet the rest of the day."

"That'll be a neat trick," Zachariah said.

"Also you're invited for supper since this is Cody's first night here."

"Won't say no to that. Your cousin's been telling me he can cook. We'll have to find out another time if he's telling the truth or just bragging."

Do you want to go over to our house now?" Jem asked Cody. She looked at her grandfather. "It's okay, isn't it?"

Before Zachariah could answer Cody told her about moving the wood. "We can play with the pups later. Let's get the job done first." Zachariah cleared his throat a couple of times which might mean he was pleased. Cody couldn't tell.

They never did get to Jem's house. Moving the wood to the back porch and stacking it just the way Zachariah wanted, took a long while. They made sandwiches and ate them out on the dock, then fooled around with some boats they made out of bark from the peeling sycamores behind the barn.

Jem kept trying to torpedo her boat with a tennis ball she'd been hitting against the barn door with a battered tennis racquet. "What do you do that's fun in the city?"

"Nothing this exciting."

"Exciting? You want exciting?" Jem scooped some candy corn out of her jeans pocket and began whizzing pieces at Cody from 15 feet away.

He stood his ground, challenging her. "Come on! Hit me!" He'd never seen a girl yet who could hit anything.

"Ouch!" One piece clipped him on the nose. She'd got lucky! He half turned and another piece grazed the side of his neck.

"That does it!" He lunged for her and tripped over the beat-up tennis racket. Jem was laughing so hard, she fell down.

Cody tried to stay mad, but couldn't. Jem was like one of the puppies. Pesky. She'd drive him crazy if he let her.

"Later," he promised. "I'll get even later." Jem just kept laughing.

Afterward Zachariah found some more small chores he wanted done. They picked up tree branches he'd pruned and helped weed around the tomato and pepper plants.

Cody was enjoying himself as Jem talked away. Once or twice he thought about Tucker Hubbard, but he was able to push him out of his mind.

Zachariah interrupted every now and then to give new instructions or tell a story as he pointed out the different rows of sweet and hot pepper plants.

"Once when Charlotte and Zack Jr. were small, a bit bigger than Timothy, they sampled some hot ones I had drying in the barn. Charlotte rubbed her eyes after touching them.

"Eek." Jem clutched her throat. "What did you do?"

"Not much we could do. Put wet cloths on your mama's eyes and they both drank lots of cold water."

When they'd finished all the work, Zachariah surprised Cody by paying them both. He hung back. His mother had told him to help his grandfather whenever he could and she wouldn't like him taking anything for it. But Zachariah simply took his hand and put the money in it.

Jem left to watch Timmy, and Cody went in the kitchen and got some orange juice out of the refrigerator. Except for Tucker, the day had been better than he'd expected. Cody took a long drink, letting the sweet, icy liquid slide slowly down his throat. He'd just have to watch out for the jerk.

Chapter 5

As he replaced the juice jug, Cody spotted something new on top of the refrigerator. A glass bowl, the color of rubies, caught light from the window and winked at him. Carefully he lifted it down.

The sides looked as if someone had pressed them in with a thumb, like something he'd seen once in the museum. He traced the indents with his finger, then put it back and went upstairs to wash and change his clothes.

He was about to go downstairs when he glanced at the closed door to the back bedroom. Zachariah was still out in the barn. Now he could have a good look.

There was a stuffy smell to the small room. Bunk beds stood against one wall with a chest of drawers opposite it. Boxes of books and papers were stacked on the bottom bunk. This had to be his father's old room. He went in to take a better look when he heard the screen door slam followed by a loud crash. Cody's heart sank as he realized what had happened.

He scooted down to the kitchen where Zachariah was sweeping up pieces of the reddish glass bowl. He looked up. "Know anything about this?"

"Yes." Cody's knees wobbled as he stopped to hold the dust pan so his grandfather could sweep the shards of glass into it. Cody dumped it into the trash basket and looked at Zachariah, waiting for the storm to hit.

"Well?"

"I thought it was pretty the way the sun sparkled through the red glass. I took it down to look at it and when I put it back, I must have left it too close to the edge."

Cody slid his hand into his jeans pocket and brought out the money Zachariah had paid him. He held it out to him. "It must have been valuable. I have some more money upstairs I brought with me. And I'll work this summer to pay for the rest of it."

"Put your money away. Your grandma liked to put fruit in that bowl. Charlotte was talking about it the other day, and I got it out to take over to her.

"I'm sorry," Cody said, feeling sick to his stomach. Would his mother think him a baby for calling her the first day he was there?

"Are you ready to go over to your aunt's for supper?"

"Yes."

"Go cool your heels on the porch then while I get cleaned up. And try to stay out of trouble."

Cody sat on the back steps for what seemed like a long time, staring up at the deer lick, waiting for the sick feeling to go away.

When his grandfather was ready, they started across the road. Zachariah didn't lock the doors or even close them. It was another reason why Cody's mother, who was city born and bred, wouldn't have felt comfortable here.

"Cody!" Jem ran to meet them. She and her father, who was holding a quiet Timmy, had been waiting for them on their front porch. She took Cody by the arm. "This is my dad, your Uncle Rob."

Uncle Rob towered over the rest of them, a nice smile lighting up his thin face. He shook hands with Cody. "We've been waiting for you to come, Cody. Especially your Aunt Charlotte. She and your father were very close."

"Fought like cats and dogs when they were young," Zachariah said just as Aunt Charlotte came out from the kitchen carrying a long-handled ladle.

She laughed. "True. We never got along until we were in high school. Zeke and I had some royal battles."

Cody frowned. "You called my dad Zeke?"

"Instead of Zack. Because he hated me making fun of his name. Then Zeke Zack, a play on zigzag." She smiled, a faraway look in her eyes. "It doesn't sound very funny now. After a while it became my special name for him and he liked it."

"What did Uncle Zack call you?" Jem wanted to know.

Zachariah chuckled. "Charlie. And did that create a ruckus. She used to pull his hair out by the handful."

"I think Charlie is sort of cute," Jem said.

"So do I," Uncle Rob said. "Is supper just about ready? I could eat a horse, Charlie."

"Horsey, horsey. I could eat a horsey, Charlie," Timmy mimicked."

"Horsetail soup is what you birds will get if you're not careful," warned Aunt Charlotte and waved the ladle at them. "Come on, Cody. You lead the way. Maybe if we feed this bunch, it'll settle them down."

A steaming bowl of chicken and gravy was already on the dining room table. A basket of still warm, baking

34

powder biscuits and a bowl of fluffy, mashed potatoes flanked it along with some new peas Zachariah had sent over earlier.

Cody sat next to Jem across from his grandfather and Timmy. Uncle Rob, at the head of the table, led them in the blessing.

"Just like your mama made, Charlotte," Zachariah said with satisfaction and took two of the biscuits, splitting them and putting one on Timmy's plate.

"I hope you're being careful about what you're cooking for yourself, Dad. You're paying attention to what the doctor said?"

Zachariah didn't bother to answer, just scowled as he ladled gravy and chicken on Timmy's biscuit.

Uncle Rob turned to Cody, taking the attention off Zachariah. "Jem tells me you had a look at Turtle Rock today. Tell me, what does a city boy think of our small town?"

"It's easy to walk around," Cody said.

"That reminds me. When we heard you were coming, I dusted off my old bike. Pump up the tires and you can ride, instead of walk."

"Thanks." Cody smiled at Uncle Rob. He was easy, laid-back, a nice change from Zachariah. "I have a bike at home. Pell bought it for me. I was wishing I had it here."

Aunt Charlotte cleared her throat, said carefully, "About Pell. You and your stepfather get along okay?"

"Really good." Cody looked around the table, eager to reassure his aunt, wanting them all to know how things were at home. "He wants to adopt me." There was a silence. "So we can be a real family."

"Zachariah who was taking a sip of iced tea, started sputtering and coughing.

"*Adopt you?*" said Aunt Charlotte, her words barely

audible.

"Yes. He said...Pell said that with the new baby coming he thought it important that I know...that I know..."
Cody stopped, started again. " He said if I had the same
last name..."

Zachariah got his voice back. "*Change your name?*"
His face, bright red when he choked on the tea, was now
colorless. Aunt Charlotte pushed back her chair, and grab-
bing the still full biscuit basket, ran into the kitchen.

Chapter 6

"Jem, I want you and Cody to take some supper over to old Mrs. Olson." Aunt Charlotte, calm once more, came from the kitchen with a foil-covered plate. "She's just out of the hospital and she always loved Grandma's chicken and biscuits."

Cody quickly pushed his chair from the table, eager to make his get-away. After he'd told them about Pell's offer to adopt him, they had eaten in silence. Even Timmy had been quiet. As they made their way through the back-yard and field to the street below, Zachariah was cutting across the road to the barn.

Jem looked at Cody. "Grandpa's probably going to hoe a row or two of weeds before dark. That's his way of letting off steam."

"He always seems to be mad about something."

Jem stopped so suddenly that Cody bumped into her. She turned around, her face flushed, her voice indignant.

"How would you feel if your only grandson was going to let himself be adopted out of the family and take another name?"

"The only grandson? What about Timmy?"

"His first grandson then. But the only one with his last name...with all his names. When he dies, there'll be no more Spains."

"Die? He's not worse is he?" An unexpected shiver went through Cody.

"I don't think so. but when he does die, there'll be nobody..."

"He doesn't care if I have his name or not. In fact, he'd rather I didn't...He doesn't think of me as real family, not like he does you and Timmy..."

"Grandpa does..." Jem began, but Cody, who'd taken all he could for one day, shouted her down.

"He hates me! Me and my mother and all the people who don't look or think the way he does."

Jem stopped again. "Cody Spain! You can't think that...that he's..."

"Prejudiced?" Cody finished for her. "Do you ever listen to him? I mean really listen?"

Jem paused. "Okay, so sometimes he shoots off his mouth. But you can talk one way and feel another. Why do you think he wanted you to come here so much? Why do you think he's been trying for the last three years to have you come visit for the summer?"

When he didn't answer, Jem demanded, "Aren't you going to say anything?"

"What's there to say?" Cody looked off in the distance. "It was your mother that wanted me to come. He didn't."

"That last part's not true."

"It is so." Cody kicked a rusty tin can hidden in the weeds. "He doesn't talk to me except to give orders or complain or say something dumb about 'you people' as if everybody with brown or black skin was alike."

Jem frowned. "Maybe...Maybe he's afraid."

"Afraid? Of Me?"

"Not afraid of you, stupid," she shot back. "Afraid of...well, the whole thing. Here he's been wanting you to come for years and Aunt Van kept saying no. Now you're here and maybe he's thinking if he says the wrong thing, you're going to go back home or hate him or..."

"You don't think he can do anything wrong, do you?" Cody interrupted.

"Of course I do. He's a human being. He makes mistakes like anybody. Like me. You've been mad at some of the dumb things I say, too, but you don't stay mad."

Cody shrugged. Zachariah was no kid. He should know better. And it was more important what Zachariah said and thought than what other people did or didn't. He was his grandfather for crying out loud. If your grandfather didn't know how to act, didn't know what hurt you, who did?

"Hey, look." Jem jabbed him with her elbow. "That's where Tucker Hubbard's grandmother lives." She pointed to a small white house, set far back from the street. "Somebody's out."

"It's Tucker," Cody said. He could feel his fists clenching and quickly he stuck them in his pocket.

"There's his grandmother. Walk fast so she won't notice us. She'll call us up and introduce us to her dear Tucker. She thinks he's an angel."

Cody didn't want any trouble, but he wasn't going to run either. A screen door slammed. Mrs. Hubbard was going back inside and Tucker was racing down the long front lawn to the sidewalk.

"I warned you," he bleated. He looked straight at Cody. "I don't like black people walking in front of my house."

He looked bigger and stronger than he had at the lake.

"And I don't stand for punks telling me what to do," Cody said, his heart hammering.

"And besides it's not your house. It's your grandmother's," Jem said.

Tucker took a step toward them just as the screen door slammed again. This time it was Tucker's father, staring straight at Cody.

Jem yanked on Cody's sleeve. "Come on, Cody, let's walk up to the deer lick before it gets dark."

Slowly he turned his back on Tucker and started toward Zachariah's.

"Remember what I said," Tucker called. "I'll be watching for you."

For once Jem was silent. They made their way home, then cut through the yard to go up to the deer lick. The block of salt was situated in a clearing to the left of the stand of pines, the land posted with "No Hunting" signs. They plopped down against a knobby tree trunk.

"What are you going to do about Tucker Hubbard?"

Cody shrugged, hoping Jem couldn't tell that talking about Tucker made him nervous. "Whatever I have to."

"Are you going to fight him?"

"Depends."

"Grandpa won't like it."

Cody shrugged again. Zachariah didn't like anything Cody did so what difference would it make?

He had trouble going to sleep that night. It was too quiet and there were no street lights. When he switched off the lamp, the room was black and as cold as death. Shivering, he pulled up the extra blanket at the foot of his bed and huddled under it. When he did sleep, he dreamed about the room down the hall with the bunk beds and the boxes of old papers. When he took the boxes off the beds, Tucker Hubbard jumped out at him, waking him. It took him a long time to get back to sleep.

The next morning he mentioned the bedroom at the breakfast table. "I opened the last door down the hall and looked in..."

"And?" Zachariah's face and voice were stony.

"It looks like a boy's room...with the bunk beds..."

There was a long silence. Zachariah was staring through the window up at the mountain. "What's your point?" he asked without looking around.

"I was thinking it's smaller, just right for me, and the bedroom I'm in would be empty in case you got company..."

"You're the first company I've had in years." Zachariah pulled out a cast iron frying pan from the drawer beneath the stove, making a lot of clatter. "The small room's too cluttered."

"I could clear it out. Or just stack the boxes at one end of the room. "I don't need a lot of space," he persisted as he watched the storm clouds gather on his grandfather's face. "It was my dad's room wasn't it?"

"You stay put where you are!" Zachariah slammed the frying pan onto the front burner. "How many eggs do you want?"

No longer hungry, Cody was ready to run, but the sound of footsteps on the back porch kept him in his chair.

A woman, her plaid shirttail flapping in the breeze, let herself in. Cody noticed her curly, rust-colored hair was the same shade as her men's pants.

"Morning, Zack." Smiling at Cody, she came straight to the table and put down a plate of chocolate chip cookies in front of him.

"I'm Maxine Purdy," she said. "Welcome to Turtle Rock." Then before Cody could thank her, she turned toward the stove.

"Eggs! I guessed you weren't following doctor's orders, Zack. One egg a week, Doc said. Charlotte filled me in."

Zachariah glared at her. "You already welcomed the boy with an apple pie, remember?" He cracked several eggs into the pan.

"Of course. Made the cookies for the Baptist bake sale. Thought a few wouldn't come amiss over here." She glanced back at Cody. "Well, go ahead and have one." She leaned in closer. "Will you look at those eyelashes? A foot long. Going to have a heartthrob on your hands here, Zack."

Cody cringed, took a cookie and ate it in two bites. Max was some kind of baker. They were loaded with chocolate chips. "They're real good, Mrs. Purdy. So was the pie. Thank you."

"Name's Max. And you're welcome. Came to see how you fellows were making out before I run over to Roulette to visit Aunt Annie and my cousin, Louise.

Max looked at Cody. "You settling in okay?" Cody nodded. "Glad you're here. Your grandpa needs company. Somebody to watch what he eats, too. See you fellows later." She let herself out.

Zachariah snorted and shoveled a crisp, glistening mass onto a plate and banged it down in front of Cody.

"For me?" Cody sniffed the scorched eggs. "I'm not very hungry now."

"No wonder, stuffing your face full of cookies. Woman ought to mind her own business!" Zachariah stomped out to the porch. Cody jumped as the screen door slammed. So this was peaceful country living.

He got up to the dump the mess into the garbage pail, but the yellow globs stared up at him, sinister, telltale. "The curse of the evil eggs," he muttered.

Checking to make sure Zachariah wasn't headed back,

he carried the plate into the small bathroom off the laundry and scraped the mess into the toilet, flushing it quickly. "Take that and that, you yellow-eyed monsters!" Listen to him. This place was driving him bonkers.

The bang of the screen door caused his heart to slam against his breast. A riled Zachariah had that effect on him. But it was Jem, out of breath, and too excited to notice the empty plate he held behind his back.

"I just saw Max leaving. Did she tell you about the bear? Everybody's talking about it."

Chapter 7

"Nels and Petie Larsen live down on Water Street in the trailer park near the Hardware." Jem was talking so fast Cody could hardly understand her. "Petie got up early to get the baby a bottle. And there was a bear walking right down Water Street on its hind legs. It was just getting light out."

"You're kidding?" Cody slipped the egg plate into the sink and began running water on it.

"No I'm not. Ask Nels when he gets here."

"Where was it headed?"

"Petie said it cut up through the Bensons' backyard, probably going back up on the hill."

"To Devil's Den?"

"No, the Bensons live on the other side of town."

"What's this about a bear?" Zachariah came in with a handful of green onions he'd just pulled and Jem repeated the story.

"Better a bear than deer. The deer are after my Mutsu apples again. Deer pellets around all the apple trees."

"The deer like apples?" Cody asked.

"Their *favor-ite*. What have you got planned?" Zachariah, no longer steamed, looked at Jem.

She frowned. " Cody, I thought we could go to Devil's Den, but it looks like rain. If I ask Mom, she'll say no. So what'll we do instead?"

"You can do some work for me. Fence needs scraping and painting. Same pay rate. What do you say?"

"Okay with me. How about you, Cody?"

"Okay. But what about Devil's Den?"

"Maybe tomorrow or the next... Oh, I forgot to tell you. Next weekend's the Fourth and Dad says we're all going to East Branch dam for a picnic and water skiing with the Gustafsons. Dad works with Mr. Gustafson in the office at Quaker State. Can you water ski?"

"I never have." But, he'd always thought he'd like to try it.

"You'll pick it up fast. Nothing to it." Jem was nothing if not self-assured--not only about herself, but Cody, too, it seemed.

"You two going to stand around jawing all day or you going to scrape fence?"

"We'll paint," Jem said.

"You've got to scrape first, Miss," her grandfather reminded her.

"We will. Oh, Grandpa, Mom wants to know if you'll watch Timmy this afternoon here. Cody and I'll help. Mom wants to go to Olean to look for a dress for her high school reunion."

"As long as you two stick around. Scrapers are in the barn. You know where, Jemma. Get them and meet me at the fence. I'll show you the section I want done."

Cody liked the barn. It was cool and airy and smelled

of sawdust and pine. "Guess this would make a good place to live." He studied the place as Jem looked for the scrapers.

"Mom says she's not in any hurry to move out of our house. But Grandpa's rooms are larger and I could have one of the big bedrooms." She looked at Cody. "Do you have your own bedroom at home?"

"Yes." He gave her the look.

"Well, how am I supposed to know? The only black people I know about are on TV. They're all either poor or rich--nobody in between."

"We're not poor and we're not rich. Just like your family. Pell has a good job with an insurance company and Mom just stopped working a month or so ago. They've been saving for a house because we're going to need a room for the baby."

When Jem didn't say anything he changed the subject.

"I looked into my dad's old bedroom this morning. At least I think it was my dad's."

"The back one with the bunks?"

"Uh huh."

"It was Uncle Zack's," Jem said. "Up until high school at least. Then he moved into a bigger one. It's full of boxes and stuff now."

"I could move everything."

"You want to stay in your dad's room?"

"It's in the back of the house and I could look out in the early morning and see if any deer are eating the apples off the trees."

"What did Grandpa say?"

"He said to stay put where I was."

"I'll ask him."

"No!"

"Why not? You want to, don't you?"

"Yes, but I don't want to beg." Cody stopped abruptly. Zachariah had come in.

"Can't you find the scrapers, Jemma?"

"Got 'em."

"Well let's get moving before it starts to rain. Clouds moving this way."

Jem did more talking than scraping. "Nels' baby is adorable."

Cody just scraped without saying anything.

"Aren't you excited about your mother having a baby?"

"I guess."

"You don't sound very sure."

"I'm sure. It's just that there'll be a big age difference so I won't be able to do things with him. I can take care of him for my mother."

"Maybe it'll be a girl."

"Maybe."

"How will you like that?"

"Fine. As long as she doesn't grow up to ask a lot of questions." Jem stuck her tongue out at him.

"Lots of jawing go on here. Any scraping getting done?" Zachariah mopped his face with a red handkerchief. It was getting warmer and darker. "You missed a patch here, Jemma. How you doing?" Zachariah never called Cody by name unless he couldn't help it. Cody hadn't called Zachariah Grandpa yet either.

A large raindrop hit Cody in the face. Jem was already heading for the barn door. By the time he and Zachariah made it to the barn, the rain was pelting down. It quieted to a gentle patter within minutes and Jem began campaigning to use the saws.

"How about Cody? Can he try something, too?" Zachariah didn't answer and Cody was glad he hadn't asked himself and been refused.

He stroked a length of pale, reddish wood propped on

the workbench. Freshly sanded, it felt as smooth and silky as one of the pups. If Zachariah had said yes to his using the tools, Cody would have made something for his mother. She wanted a small decorative shelf for the kitchen to hold a pot of ivy and the rosebud teapot he'd given her for her birthday.

"That's a piece of cherry." Zachariah took it from him.

"I like the way it feels and smells," Cody muttered, determined not to let his hurt show.

Zachariah smoothed the wood with rough fingertips. Not looking at Cody, he said, "You'll have to learn how to use the saw first on some scrap lumber."

Startled, Cody look at his grandfather. Was it possible he was softening? The answer came all too soon.

"Wouldn't hurt you to learn something useful," he said, as if Cody had wasted his life so far. "Here's some pine. You can trace the pattern for the birdhouse on it and then start cutting."

Cody took it eagerly, refusing to let Zachariah's words sting. He looked at the pattern pieces. The front had a tiny hole in it. "What kind of bird is this for anyway?"

"Bluebirds. Were pretty rare around here, then I came across this pattern the Conservation Department's been promoting. I started building houses and the birds are coming back."

"I like building stuff," Cody murmured. "It's fun and useful."

"That's what Zack Jr. used to say." A dark look crossed Zachariah's face, his mouth screwed up all small and tight as he turned away.

Chapter 8

"I'm hungry. Who wants a sandwich?" Jem, who had been going through some patterns for Christmas ornaments, interrupted Cody and Zachariah at the workbench. "I'll make them."

"Sounds good to me." Zachariah began sweeping up sawdust. The rain had stopped, the sun shining through the barn windows.

They sat at the picnic table on the back porch so they could watch the hummingbirds make dizzying attacks on the long red feeder hung from the rafters. Cody also spotted a bluebird enter one of the houses near the apple trees.

Jem handed around the sandwiches. "I made yours out of turkey baloney, Grandpa. Less fat."

"Thanks a lot, Jemma," Zachariah said, making a face.

Cody who'd had only chocolate chip cookies for breakfast was hungry. He picked up his sandwich, resisting the temptation to inspect the inside. Turkey baloney didn't sound appetizing to him either. He'd seen Jemma squirting yellow mustard happy faces on the meat, but hadn't looked closely.

"Don't worry, Cody," Jem said as he took a big bite and started chewing. "I made ours out of moose meat. Grandpa cooked up a lot of it before you came."

He stopped abruptly, his stomach lurching. Another of her tricks, he decided. Well she wouldn't get him this time. He kept chewing.

"Max's brother, Harold, went moose hunting in Wyoming last winter. Shipped the moose home in little white paper packages, all ready for the freezer. Loads of it." Jem paused to give Cody a big smile. "We've been eating it ever since. Casseroles, hamburgers, sandwiches. Right, Grandpa?"

"Right."

Cody put down his sandwich, his insides revolting. He'd seen those white freezer packages.

But for once Zachariah took pity on him. "Try looking inside the bread."

Cody flipped back the top slice, then replaced it. Even he knew baloney when he saw it and Jem was a whiz at dishing it out. He shot her a warning look, but she had collapsed again in a fit of giggles.

They were just finishing Max's cookies when Aunt Charlotte drove in with Timmy. She picked her way across the back porch eyeing the pile of wood, some chicken wire, containers of peat moss and a couple of buckets of prized cow manure someone had given Zachariah for the garden.

Aunt Charlotte made a face. "If your grandma could see this back porch, she'd roll over in her grave."

"Grandpa says he's got things just the way he likes them," Jem said.

"I'll bet," said Aunt Charlotte. "Where is he?" She plucked Timmy away from a tray of garlic bulbs Zachariah had spread out to dry.

"He's up in the garden," Cody told her.

"Keep Tim away from those bulbs will you, Cody-- and that open bag of peat moss. Jem, I'll put his blanket in on the rocker. He won't sleep without it. I should be home by 4."

Aunt Charlotte went up to the garden to talk to Zachariah before leaving.

"We're watching Timmy, Grandpa. Don't worry. I'm used to him moving fast," Jem reassured him when he came down to check on them.

"Keep him away from the pond. And the barn. Too many things he could get into around here." Zachariah paused. He looked at Cody. "I've been thinking about the back bedroom," he growled. "You still want to move in?"

Stunned, Cody looked at Jem to see if she had said anything, but she looked as surprised as Cody. "Yes!" His grandfather was unpredictable. Cody could never figure out where he stood with him.

"All right. Jemma can give you a hand. Take Tim with you. I want to restake a couple more of the tomato plants. When I get through, we'll rock a little. All right, Tim Boy?"

Timmy gave his grandfather his angel smile and moved from the garlic to some small seedlings in peat pots.

"Be careful with Grandpa's little trees," Jem warned.

"Timmy," Cody said, eager to start before Zachariah changed his mind. "Want to come upstairs and help me move into my new bedroom?" He glanced down at his cousin. "What have you got in your pocket?"

"Truck," said Tim, pulling out a tiny red fire engine and making deep tracks in the peat moss.

"You can play with it upstairs, okay?" Cody held out his hand and Timmy took it with his free one.

"Okay." Timmy looked down at their clasped hands, then at the one holding the engine. "Me beau-ful brown too."

"What?" Cody looked down at Timmy's hand and arm where bits of the peat moss clung all the way to his elbow. He laughed, suddenly feeling lighter than he had in days.

Upstairs he opened the door to the back bedroom slowly. Jem had taken charge of Timmy, stopping in the kitchen to get him a drink of juice.

Cody stepped inside, his heart beating double time. This was his father's room as a boy. He walked to the bed and ran his hand over the maple bedpost, then the dresser top, touching the places his father had touched. A shiver went through him. It was as if his father were in the room.

He knew now why he'd come to Turtle Rock, to a place where he wasn't wanted. It had been to find Zack Jr. And this was as close as he'd come.

He opened the windows. From here he could see the whole back of the property, the barn and pond and mountainside. Even the salt block at the deer lick. If he had a flashlight, he could see the deer when they came down off the hill at dawn to eat the apples.

He searched for evidence that his father had been there, had lived in this room. The walls were bare, the paint faded where pictures had hung. He checked the contents of the boxes on the bed.

There was a St. Bonaventure mug, some notebooks plus economics and philosophy text books with Z. Spain written inside. Nothing else. He traced the bold letters with one finger as if it were a message his father had left just for him. Some part of that other boy who had grown up to be his dad was still here. He closed his eyes wishing...

"It's stuffy in here." Jem came in, breaking the mood, and led Tim over to the bunk, moving one of the boxes to make room for him to run his fire engine over the bunk.

"It'll be all right now the windows are open." Cody picked up the biggest box and stored it in the other bedroom. Jem followed with another box with Timmy carrying a paperback that had fallen to the floor.

"Did you go through these boxes?" Jem asked.

"Just books."

Another trip apiece and the bed was cleared. "I'll gct the sheets," Jem offered. "You can take off the bedspreads. I think there's only mattress pads under them."

"I'm going to get my clothes first and put them away," he said. He was getting tired of her running everything.

Cody transferred his belongings to the dresser and on top propped a photo of his mother taken in front of their apartment.

"Is this where you live?" Jem cried. "Why it's nice. Trees and everything!"

"Even grass," he mocked. She hit out at him, but he dodged and threw a pillow at her and war broke out. She hit out at him and this time he landed another pillow on her head.

"Hey," she protested, giggling.

"That was for the candy corn and this," he belted her again, "is for the moose meat."

She giggled. "You fell for it. Mo-o-o-se meat, Cody!" He raised the pillow again, but without warning she gave a different kind of shriek.

"Timmy! Where did he go?" Jem ran out to the hall. Cody looked under the bottom bunk, then hearing a noise, went to the closet.

"In here," he yelled. He pulled the door wide open. Timmy was sitting on the floor playing with the contents of a box in the rear of the closet. As Cody bent over him, a sharp odor hit him in the face.

Jem came running and peered down at Timmy. "I was so scared. I was afraid he went downstairs and ...ugh! What's that awful smell?" She bent down. "Timmy, what's that white stuff on your chin? Are you eating something? Oh, what if it's poison?"

"Poison doesn't smell like that." Cody carefully pulled Timmy to his feet and brought him out, then felt around on the closet floor, closing his hand around several small objects.

"What is it?"

Cody made a face. "Garlic cloves. He must have had his pockets full. He's been eating it."

"Oh, Timmy, what kind of kid eats garlic?" Jem was laughing, but Cody's attention was suddenly focused on Timmy's hands.

"What's that?" he said and gently pried something round and shiny from the toddler's hands.

Jem peered down at it. "What is it?"

Cody turned the silver and glass object over in his hand, enjoying the smooth feel of it. "It's a pocket watch."

"Where did he find it?"

"There's a box in the back of the closet," Cody said without taking his gaze from the watch. The initials P.B. were engraved on the back.

Jem dragged the box out into the room. "Maybe there's other stuff in here." She went through it quickly putting more dog-eared notebooks, some pencils and a tattered road map on the floor.

"That's it. Nothing else. Let's go show Grandpa the watch and see if there's something that will get rid of the garlic smell. Timmy, come back out of the closet!"

Timmy was running his engine over the floor. As Cody brought him out, he spied something they'd missed--a railroad spike, rusty and flaking. Next to it was a red bandanna handkerchief in which it had been wrapped. He estimated the spike to be about five or six inches long.

"That's no good for anything. It should have been thrown away," Jem said, collaring Timmy.

"No way! Cody turned the spike over looking at it from every angle. "Let's find out, though, why it was saved." Cody followed them downstairs, just as Zachariah came into the kitchen.

"What's Timmy spitting out?"

"He's been chewing garlic."

"You do beat all, Timothy. Here sit up here on the counter and we'll start by giving you some parsley to eat. That ought to take away some of the odor. Bottom drawer in the refrigerator, Jemma," her grandfather directed.

But Timmy refused to eat it, wanting a cracker instead. Zachariah shook his head. "Wait until your mother gets a whiff of you."

Zachariah picked up Timmy and sat down with him in the rocker, giving him his tattered, blue blanket to hold on to. "You get moved into the other bedroom?" he asked without looking at Cody.

"Uh-huh. And we found something. In the closet. Or rather Timmy did." Cody held out the watch and then the spike.

"Well now." Zachariah took the watch in his hand. "I wondered many a time after Zack...afterward...where that watch went to. So did your grandma. It belonged to her father. Worked on the B&O over in Potter County.

"When her father died, your grandmother gave his watch to your daddy. He was a little older than you are

55

now. He took good care of it, then we couldn't find it...afterward."

"There was a red handkerchief on the floor. Maybe it was wrapped up in that," Cody said.

"What's the B&O?" Jem asked.

"Baltimore and Ohio," Cody answered.

Zachariah look surprised. "So you know something about railroads?"

"A little. What about this?" Cody handed him the spike, some of the rust flaking off in his hand." Zachariah took it, shaking his head.

"I'd forgotten all about this. Flood of '42 washed the section of track out between Wharton and Conrad."

Zachariah looked up at the mountain. "Your daddy always wanted to know more about the B&O. One time he and your grandma went back to where the track wound around the mountain above her old house in Conrad. Nothing left, of course, but the railroad bed, a few cinders. All the ties rotted and long gone.

"Zack Jr. kept poking around in the cinders, found this one spike. He bent to pick it up and your grandma started screaming. Rattlesnake not more than a few feet from where she was standing. Zack threw the spike. Just grazed the snake, but it gave your grandma time to move off."

"Uncle Zack was a hero," Jem said. "Does that mean the watch and spike are Cody's now, Grandpa?" she asked. "They were his father's and he found them."

Zachariah hesitated, handed back the spike. He ran his fingers over the watch crystal. "Not worth much. Just to the family. You know that?"

Cody nodded and Zachariah said harshly, "It's not a toy, not something to trade away when you..."

"I wouldn't!"

"...when you change your name."

56

Nobody said anything and Zachariah shifted Timmy on his lap, then held out the watch.

"Well, it's yours, I guess... It's a keepsake. Maybe a jeweler could clean it up and get it going again."

Cody took the watch before Zachariah changed his mind. "The spike?"

"You want the spike? All rusty and falling apart?"

"Even more," Cody said because his dad had found it, had thrown it and saved Grandma Gemma from a rattle-snake.

Zachariah didn't say anything. He glanced up at the mountain again. "It's yours," he said, his voice cold and distant.

Timmy began to fret. Zachariah soothed him. "Go to sleep, Tim Boy."

"Sing, 'Froggie'," Timmy urged his grandfather in a sleepy tone. Cradling Timmy closer, Zachariah cleared his throat.

Oh, Froggie went acourtin'
And he did ride.., A sword and
pistol by his side....

Jem and Cody tiptoed out as Timmy's eyelids drooped. On the back porch they could hear Zachariah as he con-tinued, throwing in an "uh huh," every now and then.

He rode up to Miss Mousie's door
Where he had often been before

Cody sat down, marveling over the finds. He turned the watch over and over in his hand. He liked the solid feel of the watch in his palm with his fingers and thumb curved up around it.

Gently he put it in his pocket, keeping his hand on it and leaned back on the stoop against the porch. Through the screen door Zachariah's voice drifted out.

And he took Miss Mousie on his knee
And he said

'Miss Mouse will you marry me?'

Cody glanced at Jem to see if she was listening. But she was picking at a scab on her knee, paying no attention to something she'd probably heard a thousand times.

Cody fit himself more comfortably against the post. Zachariah gave no hint of stopping and there seemed to be a lot of verses. Every now and then the song sounded almost familiar. Cody couldn't tell if it was the tune or his grandfather's voice that made his chest ache deep inside.

Several times he thought about getting up and going to the barn. But he didn't.

Chapter 9

Cody slept that night in his father's bed and dreamed again--this time of him. In the dream Zack Jr. was brown like Cody. Together they stood at the deer lick and watched Zachariah climbing the hill toward them. When Zachariah reached the top, Zack Jr. pulled the railroad watch from his pocket and said, "Too late. The train has left."

Zachariah growled and grunted, but Zack Jr. just shook his head and stood his ground.

The next morning Cody slid the silver watch in his jeans pocket. Whenever he felt like it he could stick his hand in and mold it to the smooth roundness.

It rained on and off during the morning preventing them from painting the fence or working in the garden.

Cody stared out the barn window. "If this weather keeps up, I'll never find an arrowhead."

"We'll go to Devil's Den the first good day," Jem promised.

They spent the morning working on the bird houses they'd cut the day before. Cody also traced and cut out a big C from the end of an orange crate using the jigsaw. "For my room."

At lunch around the kitchen table, Jem was full of plans for the Fourth of July weekend. "We're going to the Dam on Monday with the Gustafsons. And the day before, we're going to the Leone family reunion in Dubois. Daddy wants you to come, Cody. We're leaving right after church Sunday."

Zachariah who'd been making a list of things to get at the supermarket looked up at Cody at the mention of church.

"I suppose you go to your mother's church. Baptist, right?"

Cody nodded to both questions. Zachariah was silent for a minute.

"You were baptized in your daddy's church in the city. St. Mary's, I think it was. Did you know that?"

"No."

Zachariah played with his pencil, not looking at Cody. "I didn't think so."

"We usually go to 10 O'Clock Mass, but Mom says we'll have to go to the 8 O'Clock with Grandpa to get to the reunion on time," Jem broke in. "He always goes to early Mass."

"So do we," Cody said.

"Early service you mean," Jem corrected him. "Baptists don't call it Mass."

Cody sighed. She was always butting in. "No, I mean early Mass."

Zachariah looked at him. "I thought you said you went to your mother's church?"

"We do. First we walk to St. Anne's which is near our

60

apartment, and then we get the car and go to First Baptist," Cody explained, adding, "Pell goes sometimes."

"You mean your mother takes you to Mass every week?" The pencil slipped from Zachariah's fingers.

Cody nodded.

"You go to two churches every Sunday?" Jem cried. "How can you stand two sermons in one week?"

Zachariah harrumphed. He looked confused, like somebody discovering the world wasn't flat. The only noise in the room was the low hum of the refrigerator.

Zachariah found his voice. "Well...I'll just ask Max what time service is at the Baptist...I suppose we could go..."

"No need," Cody said quickly. "My mother and I just go to both to keep each other company. One church is enough."

Without warning, his grandfather pushed his chair back and went out on the porch. Through the window they could see him staring up at the deer lick as if he'd spotted something.

After lunch, Zachariah suddenly decided he'd go to Bradford to pick up a part for the television set which was on the blink. The night before Cody had gone to Jem's to watch the Pirates on TV with her and Uncle Rob. Zachariah had listened to it on the radio and had been visibly put out that Cody hadn't been content to do the same.

"Do you two want to go along?" Zachariah asked. "If you do, call your mother, Jemma. And see if she needs anything."

"If you're going to the mall, then I want to go," Jem answered. "There's a craft store there that has everything. I want a woodcarving knife of my own and the Hardware is out of the kind I want. Dad gets mad every time I borrow his." She looked at Cody, "Do you want to go?"

"Sure." Maybe he'd buy a flashlight to keep in his room to spot deer although he supposed the Hardware was the best place to look.

The ride over the hill to Bradford was a short one. As they cut off near the Quaker State refinery at Farmer's Valley, Jem pointed out the office building where Uncle Rob worked. A few minutes later she spotted a doe high on a hillside field.

"You're just teasing," Cody cried when he couldn't see it.

"I am not. You've got to keep your eyes open."

At the mall, Cody and Jem prowled around the craft shop under the overwatchful gaze of a sales clerk while Zachariah went into the Radio Shack. The store didn't carry flashlights. Maybe Zachariah had one Cody could use.

Jem paid for the knife and some balsa wood and they went out and found Zachariah in the parking lot.

"What did you buy, Grandpa?" Jem asked as Zachariah opened the Blazer tailgate to stow away some small packages.

"A part for my TV. Might want to watch a Pirates game myself now and then instead of listening to it on the radio."

"Are you going to get hooked up to cable?

"Well, Missy, not much we can get in these hills without it unless I put one of them saucers in my back yard and you're not going to find me messing up the place with one of them.

On the way back, Cody kept his face pressed to the window, hoping to spot a deer in one of the open fields on the hillside below the tree line, but no such luck.

They had just passed Quaker State when, on the upper side of the hill, he glimpsed something small, black, like a stuffed toy.

"Jem! Look!" He was shouting in his excitement. "It's a bear!"

Jem glanced up, disbelief on her face for only an instant and then she let out a whoop.

"Grandpa, it *is* a bear! Slow down. It's a cub. He's on the top of the ridge. It looks like it might fall down the side of the hill!"

But Zachariah couldn't stop. A pickup was right behind them and they were on a curve with no place to pull off. "You know the mother's not far away," Zachariah calmed her. "And, she'll have that cub toeing the mark in short order."

"It was so little," Cody said, his face pressed to the rear window, disappointed that he hadn't had a longer look as the Blazer rounded the curve.

"My first bear. How old do you think it was, Grandpa?" Jem asked.

"Well, this is the beginning of summer. I suppose no more than a couple of months."

It was Cody's first look at a bear in the wild, too. Wait until he told Jelly Belly about this.

Back in town they stopped at the supermarket. Cody noticed the pickup followed them into the parking lot. Two young guys got out and came over to them.

"Hey, Zack, we were right behind you. What'd you think of that bear cub falling down the hillside?"

The younger one, with stubble on his face, laughed, showing a gap between his yellow teeth. "That little bugger was so close I could of picked it off with my rifle. Had a perfect shot." He gave Cody a stare, raising his eyebrows.

Cody bristled, but not for himself. He could see the guy was showing off, but how could anyone even think of killing something so perfect?

"Don't pay any attention to him," Jem said under her

breath. "He's a jerk."

" Did you two bring the grocery list like I told you?" Zachariah growled and Cody knew he'd seen the look the man had given him. Jem pulled the list out of her jeans pocket.

"You two go in and get started while I go next door to the hardware. Need some more birdseed plus paint for the fence."

"Wait, Grandpa, I forgot to tell you. Mom said why don't you and Cody come for supper again tonight?"

Cody's hopes leaped at Jem's words, but were dashed when Zachariah said, "Can't eat there every night. Best we fend for ourselves." He glanced at Cody. "What do you want for supper?"

Last night they'd had a mostly vegetable casserole from Max because Zachariah was supposed to cut down on red meat. Cody had eaten a bowl of corn flakes and bananas later.

"I like just about anything--except..."

"Except what?"

"Pizza with anchovies."

"Well you won't find any anchovies leaping out at you in Turtle Rock so you can rest easy. No soul food either. So what do you like?"

"Anything..." Cody sputtered realizing Zachariah's barbs were beginning to slide right past him.

"You're a big help..." Zachariah was gathering steam.

Cody didn't want to make a scene, so quickly he said, "Hamburgers. I'll cook them."

"That sounds like fun," Jem agreed. "If Cody is going to cook, I'm going to stay for supper. Okay, Grandpa? I could make dessert." She flashed her grandfather a smile and without waiting for an answer went into the store.

Jem, and Timmy, too, Cody thought, took their grandfather's approval for granted. No matter what they

64

wanted to do.

Zachariah got out his wallet and handed Cody some money. "I'll be back after I put the paint in the Blazer. Don't forget to get the milk and juice. I don't suppose you like onion on your hamburgers?"

Cody shook his head. "Well, I do," said Zachariah, "and this is one time instant won't work. So pick out a big sweet one. Better have something green too."

Cody stuffed the money in his pocket and headed for the meat department, then the frozen food aisle where he found the green beans. His mother had shown him how to cook them with a little onion. That ought to please his grandfather.

Jem met him at the front of the store with a small box in her hands. "Did you get the extra lean beef? Grandpa's not supposed to have fatty stuff." She examined the package. "Yeah, that's good."

"What are you going to make?" Cody tried to see what he had, but she put one hand over the box front.

He moved one finger and read the contents. "Tapioca! Ugh! That stuff's like little fish eggs. They tried to serve it to us at the school cafeteria, but nobody would eat it."

"The way I make it, you'll love it," Jem said. "Grandpa does. He'll eat it all.

Cody frowned. "How about some cookies to go with it?"

"How much money did Grandpa give you?"

"Enough."

"It'll be okay with him if we get some. You can pick them out since you don't like tapioca," she added.

"Thanks so much." He found the cookie shelf and chose some Oreos. When he showed her what he had, it was her turn to frown.

"I was hoping you'd get something good like Fig Newtons."

"Fig Newtons?" Aggh!" He looked to see if Jem was kidding, but she wasn't. "Boy, have you got strange tastes."

"De Gustibus."

"What does that mean?" he demanded and moved to the cash register.

"It's short for De gustibus non est...non est... I can't remember exactly. It's Latin. Dad says it all the time. It means everybody has stuff they love and stuff they hate and they won't change just because someone else thinks it's dumb--or something like that."

Cody half heard what she was saying. A man and woman, both darker than he, had entered the store. Through the big plate window he could see their small maroon Buick and the Ohio license plates. They talked quietly to each other as they withdrew two Cokes from the upright cooler and got in the other checkout line.

Cody paid for their groceries and he and Jem met Zachariah in the parking lot, Cody handing him the change before climbing into the back seat with Jem.

Jem and Zachariah seemed fascinated as the black couple got into their car, slowly backed up and headed out of the parking lot toward Route 6.

"Why aren't there any black people living in Turtle Rock?" Jem asked her grandfather.

"I suppose," Zachariah said, "when they left the South they went to the cities where there was work.The only time there was any of them here in the hills was before World War II.

"President Roosevelt started the CCC program and brought in young men from the cities to fix roads, build bridges and replant the hills the loggers had stripped."

"Did you know any of them?" Jem wanted to know.

Zachariah shook his head. "The CCC boys pretty much kept to themselves. Mostly whites, some blacks. Had their own camps. They sometimes came into town." He turned the key in the ignition and started up the Blazer before finishing. "It was different--seeing a cluster of young blacks on the street. None of them would look you in the eye."

"Maybe they were afraid--because everybody else was white," Jem said.

"Maybe," Zachariah answered, his voice so low Cody could barely hear him. "Made some people uneasy--having...having strangers on the street."

"But nothing happened?" Cody wanted to know.

"Not so far as I know." Zachariah swung the Blazer around in a tight, grinding circle as if putting an end to the questions and started down Water Street.

As they neared the trailer park on the left, Jem pointed to a section of the road. "This is where the bear was seen the other morning, right, Grandpa?"

"According to Petie Larsen."

"But where did it come from?" Cody wanted to know.

"Could have come down either hillside--the one behind our house or the one across from it."

"Was it hungry? Why would it come down out of the hills?"

"Looking for a little entertainment I suppose. Mighty quiet up in the hills now. No hunters coming in and shooting cows and each other during the summer.

Cody laughed. He and Zachariah were alike in a lot of ways. When you came right down to it, there was only one thing that set them apart. But in his grandfather's eyes, the difference was too big to put aside.

Chapter 10

"So, Jemma," Zachariah asked as they drove over the lake bridge. "What kind of dessert are you going to fix with the hamburgers? Tonight's my lucky night. I get my supper cooked for me and it means you clean up too, right?"

"Uhhuh. It's something you l-o-o-o-ve. What's your very favorite dessert?"

"Raisin pie with chocolate ice cream," Zachariah said without hesitation. Cody's stomach flipped over. Moose meat was just the tip of the iceberg.

"Your next favorite," Jemma coached her grandfather.

"Gooseberries with fresh cream."

"Ughh." Cody managed to keep his cry of pain under his breath.

"All right, then," said Jemma patiently. "Your favorite pudding."

"That's easy." Zachariah smiled. "Prune fluff." They

had to be joking.

Back at the house, Jem called her mother for permission to stay for supper. She found a flowered apron that had been Grandma Gemma's and tied it around her waist.

"Here's one for you, too, Cody." She pulled out a green one with a ruffled bib and neckstrap.

"Nothing doing! I'm not messy when I cook."

"Neither am I," Jem said, "but I like the way it makes me feel." She put the second apron, not folded as neatly as before, back in the drawer.

Cody washed his hands at the sink and dried them on the towel before tearing open the package of ground beef. He made four large patties, molding the meat into balls, then flattening them out so they would cook evenly.

Jem was busy with the tapioca, measuring out sugar and milk and dumping it all into a sauce pan on the stove. It looked like she had used every bowl in the cupboard.

In the drawer under the range Cody found several frying pans and picked out a middle-sized one.

"We should probably set the table before I start cooking the hamburgers," he said.

Jem was cracking eggs, separating the whites into one bowl and dumping the yolks into another. "Okay." She didn't bother to look up. "Oh, darn!"

"What's the matter?"

"Some of the egg yolks got into the whites. Oh, well." She went on cracking eggs.

Cody got out three plates and silverware and glasses. He found the napkins and in the back of the refrigerator the catsup and a jar of relish. He cut the onion slices quickly so his eyes wouldn't sting too much.

Jem was using a handmixer to beat the egg whites. "They're not whipping very high," she moaned. "Because of the yolks. I spilled some more into the whites."

"Don't worry. It'll be fine." Cody hoped he was right.

He noticed there seemed to be a lot of stuff spilled on the stove and counter.

Jem brightened. "Of course it will. I guess I'd better start stirring the mixture." She put the tapioca and sugar and milk on the burner and turned the heat up.

She stirred for a while, then went back and beat the egg whites some more. "You can probably start the hamburgers now," she said in her take-charge voice. "When they're almost done, we can call Grandpa."

"Don't I smell something burning?"

Jem leaped toward the stove and began stirring the tapioca again from the bottom. Cody could see it was brown in places. "Not really scorched," she chirped.

The hamburgers were ready to be turned and he flipped them expertly so that the grease didn't spatter.

"Bit of a mess, isn't it?" said Zachariah who had come in to the kitchen. He walked over to where Jem was working. "And what's the smell?"

"The tapioca's browned a little," Jem said. Gives it more zing." She went back to her stirring and Zachariah studied the hamburgers. He sniffed, aahing appreciatively.

"Just have to wash up before I sit down," he said.

"I'll put the burgers in the buns," Cody answered, a glow spreading through him.

Jem was pouring the hot mixture from the stove into the egg whites. Cody watched her dump in half a bottle of vanilla extract.

"For extra flavor," she said when she realized Cody was looking. She put the pudding in the refrigerator, then sat down at the table, noticeably quiet.

When Zachariah sat down, Jem bowed her head and waited for the others to follow, then quickly said the blessing.

"And thanks for them who cooked it," added Zachariah. Cody chimed in with the amens.

"The onion slices are sort of thick," Cody apologized.

"Just the way I like them." Zachariah forked two big rings on his hamburger.

"The hamburgers are great," Jem enthused. "What did you put in them?"

"Worcestershire sauce. It's how my mother makes them." Cody noticed Zachariah didn't snort at the mention of his mother.

"Can you make anything else?" Jem asked.

"A couple of things," he said.

"Me, too," Jem said.

When they finished the hamburgers, Cody and Zachariah dividing the last one, Jem got the tapioca out of the refrigerator and ladled it into small dishes. There were little bits of brown scorch throughout.

Cody had been about to say he couldn't stand tapioca even when it was cooked perfectly, but he couldn't hurt Jem.

Zachariah hesitated, then took a big bite. "Best tapioca I ever tasted. The-uh-flavor really-uh-really comes through." Cody dug his spoon in.

"Best I ever tasted too," he said and made sure he didn't look up when he said it.

Jen who had been visibly tense, relaxed and took a big bite.

"Uggh!" She put her napkin up to her mouth, her eyes watering and looked at them both suspiciously.

"It's worse than anything!"

Zachariah broke first, his lips twitching. Cody was next. Jem kept her mouth tight, but then a giggle escaped. In a moment they were all roaring.

"What else have we got for dessert?" Zachariah wiped his eyes. "My sweet tooth needs feeding."

"Cody got some cookies. Where did you put them?" Jem demanded.

Cody put the Oreos on the table and all three dove in to get the tapioca taste out of their mouths, chasing the cookies down with milk.

"Reminds me of when Zack Jr. made angel food cake," Zachariah said. "Misread the recipe. Your grandma came in from the barn to find a dozen yolks in a bowl, the whites thrown away. Zack demanded to know what cream of Tar Tar was." Cody didn't know what it was either, but joined in the laughter. A knock on the door interrupted them.

Mrs. Hubbard had come to get some early vegetables Zachariah had promised. She sailed in, white hair perfectly waved, her dress fit for Sunday church. The sight of her apparently brought Zachariah back to reality. When she looked at Cody, Zachariah scowled at him, leaving Jem to make the introductions.

"This is my cousin Cody," Jem said.

"About Tucker's age. He'll be coming back for the Fourth. Family's camping this week. Smart boy, my grandson Tucker." Mrs. Hubbard's gaze was focused at a point just above Cody's head.

"Maybe Tucker'll get lost in the woods--permanently," Jem whispered in his ear as they went out to the back porch and then up to the pond. "Mrs. Hubbard's a widow. She likes Grandpa. She and Max are always bringing food to him, seeing which one can outdo the other.

"Max seems okay," Cody said.

"Yeah, but Grandpa seems to like Mrs. Hubbard more. He's always having fights with Max. Max likes to argue with him, but Mrs. Hubbard's always so sweet. I think she wants him to marry her." Jem made a face.

Later after they had cleaned up the kitchen and were headed for Jem's, they saw Zachariah sitting on the front porch with Mrs. Hubbard. She was looking up at him and smiling.

Jem made a rude noise under her breath. It was nothing to Cody who his grandfather liked or if he got married, but he thought Max was much nicer. There was something about the way Mrs. Hubbard looked at him, or rather didn't look at Cody when she spoke to him.

Uncle Rob was mowing the lawn when they got to Jem's house and Aunt Charlotte was weeding a begonia bed around the stairwell of the walk-out basement, trying to keep Timmy from pulling out flowers.

The door to the basement was open and they went in and got J.B. and Spats and brought them out to the lawn to play. Cody wished he could take J.B. back to Zachariah's and let him sleep on the bottom bunk. He could keep Cody company at night when it was lonely. The pup was so cute the way he licked Cody's hands and face with the little pink tongue. Jem said that in two weeks they could be given away.

"How was supper?" Aunt Charlotte wanted to know.

"Good," Cody said. Jem made a face and then told her mother about the tapioca including the mess she'd made cooking.

Aunt Charlotte shook her head. "I hope you cleaned it up."

"We did," Cody said. "We didn't want Max getting mad. She's supposed to come clean tomorrow."

"Mrs.Hubbard's over on the porch swing with Grandpa," Jem informed her mother. "All dressed up like she was going to a party."

"Alice was one of your grandmother's friends. It's natural she and Grandpa enjoy talking to each other."

"Well, I don't like her."

"Jem!"

"Well, I don't." Jem scowled. "She keeps looking at Grandpa as if he'd just said something amazing. And you can't make yourself like people, if you don't."

"No, but you don't have to be open about it. I hope

you don't let Grandpa hear you talk like that."

"Oh, no! I just thought of something awful," Jem whispered to Cody. "If Grandpa and Mrs. Hubbard ever got married, that nerd Tucker would be our cousin."

"Not mine, ever!"

They played with the pups a while then went inside to watch a movie about a white man who was adopted by an Indian tribe. Half way through, Cody yelled with excitement as the man let himself be tortured to prove he was selfless, a worthy member of the tribe.

"That's the Sun Vow, part of the Sun Dance," Cody exclaimed. "I read about it in my book. I'll show it to you."

"No, thanks. It's too gory," Jem said. I'd rather read about Indian crafts like..."

"Arrowheads," Cody finished for her. "Maybe we could go to Devil's Den tomorrow?"

"If it doesn't rain."

After the movie, Cody ran back home. Zachariah was reading the newspaper and it reminded Cody of something he'd heard his aunt and uncle talking about earlier.

"Uncle Rob says there's a piece in the paper about why all the bears have been sighted around here lately."

"In the sports section." Zachariah pointed to it without putting down his paper.

Cody reached for it, found the piece, and began reading to himself. The story from the Pennsylvania Game Commission reported the state's bear population was still on the rise.

"Wow," Cody said, forgetting for a moment that there was only Zachariah to talk to. "This says males can stand as high as six feet and grow up to 600 pounds. I wouldn't want to meet up with one of them."

He continued reading, half to himself, half aloud.

"'Pennsylvania's native black bears are timid creatures,

usually fleeing when confronted by humans or dogs.' I wonder if that's true?"

Zachariah's answer was the usual growl. "The key word there is 'usually'. I don't know as I'd want to fool around with a 600-pounder just to see what he's going to do."

Cody put down the paper, a shiver running through him. "Me either."

Chapter 11

Cody heard Jem slam across the front porch and through the hall. She came to a halt in the kitchen.

"Hi, Grandpa." She helped herself to a piece of toast. "You still want to go to Devil's Den, Cody?"

"What's this about Devil's Den?" Zachariah put down his manual on raised-bed gardening.

"I promised to show Cody the big rocks and he wants to find an arrowhead before he goes home. Devil's Den ought to be a good place to find one."

"So you're going home?" Zachariah sounded as if it was what he had expected all along.

Cody wasn't about to give him the satisfaction. "Not right away. I just wanted to find an arrowhead before I do go. Where I live there's not a chance. All the ground has been built on or leveled for parking lots."

"Well, I don't suppose there's any harm." Zachariah turned to Jem. "See what your mother says first though."

"We will."

Cody was putting their dishes to soak when Max came, armed with her own vacuum cleaner.

She poured herself a cup of coffee and glanced at Cody. "I heard you moved into the back bedroom. "You haven't got a toad or any other surprises for me hiding out up there have you?"

"No. How did you know that I moved?"

"Oh, I have my spies." Max winked and wheeled the sweeper into the living room. Zachariah snorted, then went to the barn, slamming the screen door behind him.

Aunt Charlotte wasn't pleased about their going to Devil's Den.

"It's perfectly safe," Jem coaxed. "Cody wants to look for an arrowhead. I think we should look in the crevices around the Flats. I'll bet we'll find some there."

"I suppose it's all right," her mother agreed. "Just don't spend all day. I don't want to have to start worrying."

"Where you going?" Timmy, with Spats in his arms, came up from the basement. "I want to go, too."

"Not this time, Timmy. Cody and I will take you for a walk when we get back--in the wagon. Right, Cody?"

"Sure," Cody said.

"With Spats." Timmy planted a kiss on the pup's head.

"Spats, too," Jem promised. "Let's go, Cody. No wait. Let's take sandwiches and something to drink. We can have a picnic up on Tabletop Rock. It's perfect. Or we can go over on the Flats. More room to spread out."

Aunt Charlotte was still fretting. "You'll be careful?"

"Promise," Cody assured her as Jem threw open the refrigerator door and then the cupboard.

"Peanut butter and jelly okay, Cody?" He nodded.

"You can get the canteen. It's down on the shelves next to where Mandy and the pups are."

"Okay." He went downstairs, moving slowly past the puppies and Mandy. J.B. scampered over to him as if he knew Cody.

"Sweet, isn't he?" Aunt Charlotte had come downstairs to put Spats back with the other puppies. She looked from Cody down to J.B. "I asked Grandpa if you could have one, but he said, no, there was no use your getting attached to a dog because you probably couldn't keep it in the apartment. Is that right?"

Cody nodded. "We're getting a house by next year."

"I know. Your mother wrote me. And I know you'll have a dog then."

"I hope so."

"Well don't feel so bad. You can spend all the time you want over here playing with these." Aunt Charlotte sighed. "It's unlikely we'll be able to find homes for them all right away. And I don't think Timmy is going to let us give Spats away." She went to the shelf and found the canteen and handed it to him.

"Thanks." He started up the steps and turned back. "Thanks, Aunt Charlotte for asking...if I could have a dog...even if it didn't work out." He hurried up the steps.

"Give me that." Jem grabbed the canteen and filled it with lemonade, slopping a little on the floor. Cody got a paper towel and wiped it up. "We don't want to bother with cups. You're not fussy about germs are you?"

"No."

"Me neither, but Mom is, so let's go before she comes up and notices we're not taking any." Jem yelled goodbye down the steps to her mother and they went across the road to Zachariah's. He was working in the garden.

Jem waved to him and held up the lunch bag and canteen so he could see. "Back in a couple of hours."

"Watch yourselves. No crazy stuff," he called to them.

They began climbing the hill. Cody had found Devil's

78

Den on a state map, the elevation 2200 feet. Such heights seemed like mountains to him, but people in Turtle Rock called them hills.

It wasn't long before they were into the pines, the ground slippery with fallen needles. Cody breathed deeply, enjoying the scent of the evergreens. Shafts of light studded with dust motes shone through the branches, making golden circles on the forest floor.

Jem was moving too fast to pay attention. Cody supposed this was old stuff to her. He breathed deeply again, filling his lungs with the clean smell. It always surprised him to see how fast Jem could move.

"Devil's Den is a little to the right," she said. "Let's start cutting over." It was quiet in the woods, the sound of truck traffic from Route 6 a muffled roar.

"Do you think we'll see some deer?"

"If they don't smell us coming." They were out of the pines now, in a forest of hardwoods.

Jem, ahead of him, was pointing down at the ground. "See this hole. Woodchuck. Don't step in it or you'll break an ankle and I'll have to carry you down the hill."

"Ha! You couldn't even pick me up."

"Oh, can't I?" She advanced threateningly, then started laughing. When he gave her a look, she said, "You're funny, Cody."

"And you're touched in the head," he retorted. "Look at that tree trunk." A perfect fan-shaped fungus, a foot in width, grew out from the base of the tree. He stooped to touch it and discovered it was hard which surprised him. It looked mushroom soft.

They moved steadily upward and crossed a small mountain stream gurgling downhill over the hollowed-out route of dirt, rocks and dead leaves.

Jem unhitched the backpack with the sandwiches and bent over. Lying on her stomach she took a long drink.

She came up with her face all wet and Cody started laughing.

"Let's see you do better," she challenged.

He leaned over, not wanting to get wet and knelt on a flat rock, putting down the canteen which he had slung over his shoulder. He scooped up water with his hands. It was cold and delicious and tasted better than anything he'd ever drunk in his entire life.

He bent over to take another mouthful. "Watch out for that snake," Jem murmured. He grinned and scooped up more water, drinking it greedily. She was always putting him on. This time he wouldn't fall for it.

Then out of the corner of his eye, he saw the small black snake swimming toward him. He jerked and went down on one elbow into the water. He reared back and gave Jem a look. She doubled over with laughter as the snake swam away.

He was ready to let her have it when he spotted something. He brushed aside a damp leaf with his foot. Even in the dim woods he could tell the small, flat stone was a beauty. Three inches across, its fossil imprints of tiny sea shells stared up at him. He picked it up, exulting. So this mountain top had been under water once.

He passed the stone to Jem who had her hand out."Do you realize," he said," that we're the first human beings to touch it? This stone has been lying there millions of years waiting for us to discover it."

"Wow! It's hard to believe," she said and turned it over, running her finger over the shell indentations. "Flat and round, just the size of Max's chocolate chip cookies." She grinned and handed it back.

Cody put it in his left jeans pocket. The watch was in the right pocket. He patted it through the jeans material. Zachariah would be mad if he knew Cody had brought the watch up here, but he'd make sure nothing happened to it.

They continued upwards making their way over fallen trees. Cody picked up a thick branch and whacked it against a tree trunk to shorten it for a walking stick, then had to wait while Jem did the same. They walked more slowly, the sticks hampering their progress instead of helping. They had been climbing for about 45 minutes when, out of breath, they came to a dirt road.

"It's the old logging road," Jem explained. It starts in a farmer's field a couple of miles from our house. Most people don't know it's there."

"You mean you could drive up here?"

"Grandpa could with his Blazer this time of year. Not in the winter. It takes 4-wheel-drive even in good weather because it's rough and there are so many ruts."

Beyond the road there was a clearing and in its center the first boulder, big as a small house. Somebody had painted a red devil's head on the side. On the south side, a small fir tree grew out of a crevice in the rock. Beyond were more boulders, tipped in all directions, sometimes two of them joining to form a cave.

"Wow!" He'd had no idea it would be like this. To think it was on top of a mountain in a small town where few people saw it or even knew about it. "How big is this place?"

"I'm not sure. Several acres maybe. Let's go over this way to Table Top."

They moved slowly, climbing up and through the canyon of rocks. Cody could see why it was called Devil's Den. It was a little eerie and he could see that falling between the narrow crevices would be like falling into hell. A boulder ahead of them towered at least 20 feet high in the air.

"Must have been dumped here by a glacier," he decided.

"Probably." Jem pointed to a huge rock with a slightly sloped surface ahead of them. "Here we are. We can get up on top by climbing on those smaller boulders around back."

Cody scrambled after her, their rubber-soled sneakers gripping the stone surface, and in a few minutes they had scaled it.

He felt as if he were on top of the world. Looking South, he could see a series of mountain ridges, soft purple in the distance.

"Look down under that tree." Jem pointed to a small mound of brown pellets. " That's deer. They look just like rabbit marbles, only bigger. And over there..." She pointed to another pile of animal dung. "That's bear. That's why Mom didn't want us to come."

The dung was gray, cigar-sized. "Too small for bear."

"What else would it be?" Jem demanded.

"I don't know." He thought about the newspaper article Zachariah had shown him the night before. He didn't think you had to worry about bears up here. Still he found himself looking over his shoulder every now and then.

"Up there are the Flats," Jem said and pointed to a field of huge even-topped rocks forming one big level surface. "Let's go there to eat." He followed her as she began moving higher.

"This is one of my favorite flowers." Jem pointed to bushes with shiny green leaves. "It's Mountain Laurel and in early June they're covered with tiny pink and white blossoms that look like little tea cups. I wanted to dig some of the plants up and put them around our house, but we aren't allowed to transplant them because it's the state flower."

Things, especially living things, ought to stay in their original places, he decided, then thought about himself. City born, was he trying to transplant himself?

Settling down on one of the rocks, pleasantly warm from the sun's heat, they unpacked the knapsack and pulled out the sandwiches and some cookies. Jem unscrewed the canteen and passed it to Cody. The lemonade was icy cold and almost as good as the water from the stream. Jem drank next and wiped her mouth with her sleeve.

"What's down the back side of the mountain?" Cody asked.

"Irish Hollow. There are a few houses down there. Once I came up with some kids from school. We got turned around and went down that way by mistake. It took forever to walk home and Mom wasn't too happy."

Cody helped himself to some cookies and leaned back on one hand enjoying himself. It was great. Like being on top of the world. He stuck his hand in his pocket and felt the watch, took it out and looked at it.

Jem watched him. "What are you thinking?"

"Oh, just wondering what my dad thought when Grandma Gemma gave this to him. It seems wrong I'll never know."

"Yeah, sometimes I can hardly wait to die."

"What!" Sometimes Jem said the nuttiest things. "Why?"

"Because we'll all be in heaven and we'll get to talk to all the people who've died. You'll get to know your father and you can ask him all the important things you want to. I've got a whole list of people to talk to when I die."

Cody grinned. She was crazy. "Who?"

"The people in Pompeii to see what it was like when Vesuvius blew and the guys who built the pyramids--the workers, not the kings. And my great-great-great-grandmother Vittoria who came to this country in the hold of the ship because one of her babies had diphtheria and they were quarantined and..."

"Yeah, yeah," he said to cut her off. He thought about telling her about the slave ships, but he couldn't bear thinking about how bad those trips had been, about people being forced to come to a place they hadn't wanted to and about all the ones who hadn't made it.

Cody wasn't eager to die. He bet his dad hadn't been either. There was too much to see and do first.

"Let's go look for arrowheads," he said. They scrambled down the hard surface, heading back for the big rocks by the road where there was more open land.

They came to two huge rocks which leaned into each other forming a cave. Inside, they spotted a small hole in the back where the rocks didn't meet. The floor was covered with dead leaves.

"What's this cave called?" Cody asked.

Jem shrugged. "You can name it."

He grinned, enjoying himself. "Okay. It's Cody's Castle."

They sat in front of the cave, Cody playing with the watch, holding it by the crown of the stem.

"Let me see it," Jem asked.

Reluctantly he put the watch into her hand. If Zachariah knew he'd brought it up here he'd be in trouble. A sound made him look up. Some distance above them a mother deer and twin fawns were grazing.

Cody drew in his breath. He'd never seen anything so beautiful. The babies had white spots on their orangish brown coats which gleamed like copper in the sun.

"Jem!" he alerted her in a hushed voice. They got to their feet slowly. Carefully they picked their way up toward the deer, dropping down on their stomachs to watch.

"I wish I had a camera," Jem said. The deer began to move. They followed, hiding in the grass for a long time, unable to tear themselves away.

Without warning, thunder rumbled across a sky that had turned from bright blue to gray while they were watching the fawns. The doe moved into the woods, the babies right behind her.

"We'd better start down," Cody said. "It's going to pour." At Cody's Castle they grabbed their belongings, the thunder crashing in their ears.

They had gone several yards down the hill, sliding over the leaves still wet from other rains, when Cody remembered.

"My watch! Let me have it."

Jem put her hand in her pocket, slowly pulled it out. It was empty.

"Oh, no! I put it in here when we moved to watch the deer. It must have fallen out."

"Then I'm going back up!"

"You can't! Not in the thunderstorm."

"I don't care." Cody turned and started up, when a crash of thunder shook the forest and the rain came down in buckets.

"We can go back tomorrow and find it," Jem pleaded. "We can't look now. Lightning might hit us. Please don't be mad at me, Cody. Please!"

Chapter 12

"Please say something, Cody." Jem continued to plead with him as they raced down the mountain. "I didn't mean to lose the watch. We can go back tomorrow to look for it."

Cody refused to answer, keeping a few feet behind her most of the way. As they cut across the stand of pines, thunder and lightning put on a fierce show making them sprint all the way to the barn. By the time they reached the back porch, where Aunt Charlotte waited with Zachariah, they were drenched.

"Thank goodness!" Aunt Charlotte greeted them. "The storm came up so fast it took us all by surprise. I'm glad you had sense enough to come right down."

Neither answered. Zachariah didn't seem to notice, but Aunt Charlotte looked from one to the other as if trying to figure out what was going on.

"Both of you have to get out of those wet clothes,"

she ordered.

"I'm not cold," Jem said and sneezed loudly.

"Here." Aunt Charlotte thrust a pair of jeans and a shirt in Jem's hands. "I figured you'd need a change of clothes. Use the downstairs bathroom. Cody, you'd better go upstairs and find something dry."

Without looking at anyone, Cody went inside, careful not to let the screen door slam. Jem was right behind him. She followed him to the bottom of the stairs. "Cody, we'll go tomorrow to look. I'll find the watch. I promise."

He refused to turn around or answer her. He was as angry with himself as he was with Jem for losing it. In his bedroom he propped up the fossilized stone where the watch had been.

By the time he came back downstairs, the rain had stopped and Jem and Aunt Charlotte had left. Zachariah was in the rocker, making notes in a garden journal. Cody tried the TV. Until the cable hookup was made, all he could get was snow. He went back upstairs to his room and picked up the book about Indian rites and found the section on the Sun Dance and Vow performed by the Plains Indians.

In one version, they hung from ropes attached to the top of a pole. At the other end of the ropes were rawhide thongs skewering their breasts and backs, the Indians hanging there until their skin broke. A shiver ran through him. It was one Indian rite Cody wanted no part of.

When he went downstairs again, Zachariah was puttering in the kitchen.

"Good night for pancakes and home fries," his grandfather said, not looking at him. "You could ride your bike to the store and pick up a quart of buttermilk. I'll get started peeling potatoes."

Cody jumped at the chance to do something. He went

upstairs to get money to buy a comic book at the grocery. It looked like it was going to be a long evening.

Instead of reading, he wound up listening to the Pirates with Zachariah, thankful his grandfather didn't make some comment about his staying home.

The next morning he went to Mass with the whole family. Jem, Timmy and their parents left right after church for the Leone reunion. Cody thanked Uncle Rob for asking him, but said he'd rather stay home. If he got a chance he was going back up to Devil's Den and look for the watch.

He never got it. Zachariah decided to work in the barn and told Cody to work on his birdhouse. "Keep you out of trouble," he said. "I don't want to have to start wondering if you drowned yourself up at the lake or are doing something else you shouldn't."

When Cody started to nail together the birdhouse, he had to ask for help. Without conversation, Zachariah held the parts while Cody nailed together the upright oblong box with slanted top.

When he was done he reached for a can of red paint. Zachariah shook his head.

"What color should I paint it?"

"Bright blue like the males. It'll attract the lady bluebirds," Zachariah growled.

Cody noticed that every time Zachariah turned half way friendly he caught himself as if he didn't want Cody to get the wrong idea about wanting him there.

When Cody put the birdhouse aside to dry and began eyeing the length of promised cherry, Zachariah shoved a worn packet of patterns toward him.

He picked out a simple shelf pattern and spent the rest of the afternoon tracing it on to the wood. Then using the jigsaw he cut out the curved end and back pieces. He worked very slowly to make sure he didn't ruin the wood.

Zachariah worked on the swing, every now and then whistling some tuneless bit.

It was not exactly what you would call a sociable time, not like when Cody and Pell did something together, but at least Zachariah wasn't yelling at him every minute.

Max came late in the afternoon with some food and invited herself for supper. Cody was glad for some company. Not only did Max get the meal ready, but insisted on cleaning up. Cody helped her wipe dishes and they asked each other riddles while Zachariah sat on the back porch.

Max's riddles were pretty awful. "What do pigs put on their sunburns?" she asked.

He shook his head, laughing.

"Oinkment."

"Aggh."

Max grinned. "Here's another one. Why did the goose lay the golden egg?"

"I don't know. Why?"

"She hated polishing silver."

"Double aggh!"

"Let's see you do better."

Cody was ready. "Why was 6 afraid of 7?"

"Why?"

"Because 7, 8, 9."

"Yipes, cannibalism."

"Over their laughter, Cody could hear Zachariah snorting as if he resented anybody having fun.

It was hard to tell Max's age. Older than Aunt Charlotte and younger than Zachariah was his best guess.

"Quiet day without Jem and the rest around," Zachariah muttered at bedtime.

"It was okay," Cody answered, but he was looking forward to the next day when they were going to East Branch Dam with the Gustafsons who lived up Bloomster

Hollow. Mr. Gustafson worked with Uncle Rob and had two boys about Cody's age.

The next morning was perfect, hot and dry. Cody figured the pond would soon be warm enough to swim in.

Uncle Rob and Aunt Charlotte were in the driveway before 10, their van loaded with ice chests. Jem got out to ride with Cody and Zachariah in the Blazer.

"We had a great time yesterday. What did you do, Cody?"

"Worked on the shelf," he mumbled without looking at her.

He could feel her staring at him and then suddenly she got back in the van.

Zachariah glanced at him but didn't say anything as they climbed in the Blazer and guilt washed over Cody. Later that day he promised he'd apologize to Jem for the way he'd acted.

The route to the Dam in neighboring Elk County was almost all on dusty back roads. Red-winged black birds perched on broken rail fences and black-eyed Susans grew in abandoned fields of crooked apple trees.

Once they stopped to get spring water from a small pipe sticking out of the hillside. Zachariah filled a gallon jug for making coffee. The van was already parked near the boat ramp when they arrived. Mr. Gustafson and the two boys were aboard the docked boat ready to take them all over to the opposite shore where Mrs. Gustafson was waiting at the campsite.

Uncle Rob introduced Cody to the boys. Steve was 12 and Kyle was Jem's age. Right off Cody knew he liked Steve best. Slow talking with a big smile, he offered a hand to pull Cody into the boat. Kyle was antsy, wanting to shove off before everyone was safely in. Cody could tell they were trying not to stare.

"Ever water ski?" Kyle demanded of Cody. When

Cody shook his head, he boasted, "I can--on one foot--for hours."

Steve gave his brother a look. "He's always bragging. It's easy," he reassured Cody. "Dad will take it slow with the boat until you get the hang of it. One of us will ski first, so you can see what to do, then it'll be your turn."

"I want to try again, too," said Jem. "I just learned last year and want to practice some more."

Nobody was paying attention to her, Cody noticed, and she suddenly grew very quiet.

They piled into the boat and Cody asked lots of questions, shouting over the noise of the boat as they rounded a bend and headed toward the campsite. Mrs. Gustafson and their dog, Thunder, came down to meet them. She apologized for Laurie, 15, who was sulking over having to leave a boyfriend behind.

"Let's haul this stuff up to where the tents are, boys," Uncle Rob said. The Gustafsons were staying overnight and camping out. Cody wished he knew them well enough to be asked to stay. Jem, he thought, would love it too.

"Jem, keep an eye on Timmy for a few minutes," he heard Aunt Charlotte say and Cody, eager to explore the long stony shore and woods above, lost track of what she was doing.

The reservoir was a great place, he decided, although he doubted there was much chance of finding an arrowhead. The area had been worked over thoroughly in the making of the dam.

"We're going to ski now. Come on, Cody, you can change into your trunks up here in the woods," Steve called. He found his gym bag and followed Steve. Kyle was first to ski and began hotdogging as soon as he got up, signaling to his father to go faster and faster. Everybody grinned when he fell going to one ski.

"Your turn next, Cody," Mr. Gustafson called as the boat circled back to shore.

"You go, Steve," Cody said. "I'll watch and see how you do it."

"Okay." Steve was good too but in a less flashy way than Kyle. Then Jem wanted a turn. She got up easily and he could see how pleased she was. All the adults yelled hurrah for her, but the boys didn't, and when she looked at him, Cody pretended not to notice.

Besides, he was nervous. What if he got up and made a fool of himself after Jem, a little girl, had been able to?

He fell the first time, but everybody shouted encouragement, so he got up and tried again, and this time he was able to stay up.

Exhilaration went through him as Mr. Gustafson took the boat down the dam. He fell as he was trying to make a turn, but Mr. Gustafson circled around and Steve swam out to him to help him get back up again. By the time they all had second turns, Cody was pretty good.

"You're a natural," Steve praised him and Cody couldn't help grinning.

But then Kyle piped up. "What else are you good at? I mean sports."

"Hockey," Cody said. "We have a team."

"I didn't think you people ice skated," Kyle said and Cody saw Steve make a face at Kyle who persisted. "Well there aren't any blacks on the national hockey teams are there?"

"The Rochester Amerks did," said Cody. "And some of the others, too."

They fixed sandwiches for an early snack then went swimming. Later in the afternoon after more skiing, the men built a fire to cook hot dogs and hamburgers. When Cody told Steve he was looking for an arrowhead, the two of them went off trailed by Thunder. They searched the shore and slopes.

"Why do you want to find one?"

"I like Indian stuff. It's special." Cody told Steve about the Indian book and the Sun Dance.

"Nobody forced them to torture themselves?" Steve asked.

"Nope."

"Why would they do it?"

" Different reasons. To fulfill a vow, to give thanks to the Great Spirit. I suppose to show they were worthy to be part of the tribe."

"I can think of better ways to prove it."

Back at the camp, Cody heard Jem ask Laurie if she wanted to take a walk with her and Timmy.

"Not with babies," Laurie answered. Jem's face went bright red. Cody felt bad for her and wished he'd been nicer. He started over toward her, but she saw him coming and walked away. He helped himself to a hot dog and sat down with Steve and Kyle. After stuffing themselves with chocolate cake, they had a watermelon seed spitting contest, everyone laughing except Jem.

When it was time to leave, Steve told Cody they'd all get together to do something soon.

"You must have been awfully bored with no guys around," Kyle said.

Jem was near enough to hear him and Cody saw her mouth droop. When it was time to load up, she got in the van without looking at Cody, pretending not to hear him when he called to her.

The ride home was quiet. Zachariah who had taken a nap in a hammock the Gustafsons had strung up, yawned, looked over at Cody.

"What's going on with you and Jemma?"

Cody looked out the window. "Nothing much."

"Been cool to each other ever since you came down

from the rocks the other day."

He shrugged. Tonight or tomorrow, for sure, he'd tell Jem he was sorry and fix it up with her. The watch was something special, but Jem, he knew, was more important.

Zachariah acted like Cody was an outsider, but right from the start Jem and Aunt Charlotte and Uncle Rob, even Timmy...they'd treated him like family, like he belonged.

Chapter 13

Cody didn't get the chance to apologize to Jem the next morning.

"Jem woke up with a fever and fell asleep on the couch after breakfast," Aunt Charlotte said when she came over to borrow one of Grandma Gemma's cookbooks.

"Just a 24-hour bug probably. I hope you and Timmy don't come down with it, Cody." She tucked the cookbook under her arm. "Where's Grandpa?"

"Up by the apple trees. Some of the Mutsu branches were broken off during the night and there are a lot of green apples on the ground." Together they walked up to the tiny orchard to inspect the damage.

"Doesn't look like the deer have been at it." Zachariah shook his head, clearly puzzled. "But who'd do a destructive thing like that?" Neither Cody nor Aunt Charlotte had an answer for him.

Zachariah usually worked in the garden from early

morning until noon, hoeing and pulling weeds in the hill-side plot behind the barn. This morning Cody worked alongside his grandfather, stopping once when the mail was delivered.

There was a postcard from his mother reminding him that Pell had some meetings in Toronto and she was go-ing with him for the two-day session. She'd included the phone number of the hotel where they'd be staying in case of an emergency and said she would call Cody when they got back.

"Hope you're having a good time," she wrote, add-ing, "Pell says it's too quiet around the house and Jelly Belly keeps calling to find out when you're coming home."

Cody put the card on his dresser and left the rest of the mail on the kitchen table and went back to the weed-ing.

Cody hadn't been big on getting down in the dirt on his hands and knees to pull weeds, but after a while he took pride in the way the rows of tomatoes looked, the smell of the leaves sharp and pleasant in his nostrils. Every once in a while he'd come across a fat white grub and Zachariah would pounce on it as if it were a demon.

The sun was hot and Zachariah stopped every so of-ten to mop his face with a red handkerchief he'd tucked around his neck. He wore a straw hat to protect his fair skin and some gloves he had patched on Grandma Gemma's sewing machine. Aunt Charlotte and Jem laughed like anything when they saw them, but Cody thought it was clever the way all the fingers had differ-ent colored patches.

"Anything important in the mail this morning?"

"Postcard from my mom. A gardening magazine and bills for you."

Zachariah grunted the way he always did and fanned

96

his face with his hat. "Sun's really beating down this morning."

Cody glanced at the leathery redness of his grandfather's neck. He was glad he didn't have to worry about burning. Cody's dad had been red-haired and light-skinned too. Normally Cody was a pale tan, but after yesterday on the lake he was closer in color to the rich red brown of the peat moss Zachariah had worked into the soil.

He held up his arm to the sun, admiring the shade until he saw Zachariah watching him. He wondered how his grandfather felt about him turning even darker.

"Time for a break," Zachariah announced. "Too hot today to do much more."

Cody eyed the pond. "The air's so hot, the water ought to be warm enough to go in."

"Water's not exactly warm, but I suppose if you're determined...

"Okay!" It was what he and Jem had been waiting for, but she wasn't there to enjoy it. He hesitated for only a second then stripped down to his cut-off jeans.

"I'll be on the patio watching. Mind you, don't pull any fool stuff and you're not ever to go in alone or without an adult watching."

"I won't." He ran up to the pond watching the water trickle out of the pipe fed from the underground spring. The pond was about twenty feet across and three times that in length with a small movable dock at one end.

His gaze ran the perimeter, on the alert for dead animals. Jem had said they'd pulled a baby rabbit out last year. The sides were mucky, so was the bottom, Jem said, but at eight feet, it was deep enough so he could keep clear of it.

He dove in from the side, gasping from the icy plunge as he surfaced. It was freezing down below where the sun hadn't hit. He pulled himself up on the grass and tried it again, glancing over at Zachariah who was fanning himself under one of the sugar maples.

Cody shivered and thought he saw his grandfather smile. That would be the day! He dove in again and this time came up to grab an inner tube off the dock. It was hot from the sun. He lay across it and let the warmth of it sink into him.

"Oh, Jelly Belly, you don't know what you are missing," he muttered. He paddled to one side and found himself under the spray of the pipe. He shrieked. It was freezing. He looked up at the patio and this time Zachariah was laughing! But when he saw Cody watching him, he turned and busied himself with a hoe handle he was mending.

Cody paddled some more, toasting himself under the sun, then ducking under the freezing spray, trying to see how fast he could get in and out from under the pipe.

As he floated in the tube, he saw Alice Hubbard coming around the side of the house. Bringing more food probably.

Someone was behind her.

It was Tucker! Wearing swim trunks! So he was back.

"He's got a lot of nerve after all those threats," Cody muttered and climbed out of the water.

Zachariah motioned to him and he crossed the lawn to where the three were. Tucker had the usual big smirk on his face.

"This is Alice's grandson Tucker," Zachariah said. "He wants to swim."

"Tucker Hubbard, my son Stanley's youngest boy," Mrs. Hubbard said as if she were presenting royalty.

"We've met," Cody said, "down by the lake." He looked to see if Tucker was fazed, but there wasn't a trace of uneasiness.

Mrs. Hubbard smiled at Tucker, not even looking at Cody. "I've got potatoes on the stove about to boil over, so I'd better go. Enjoy yourself, Tucker."

Tucker didn't answer, didn't wait for Cody or even look at him, but ran across the yard and dove in the pond without checking to see how deep it was or anything else. Cody moved to the dock. Tucker surfaced, swam up to him and cut a spray of water which hit Cody in the face.

Cody blinked, anger growing. "You shouldn't just dive in without checking to see if there's anything you could hit your head on," he said, trying to hold his temper.

"I swam in here lots of times last year, even in the middle of the night," Tucker bragged. "Sneaked out of the house. I was here last night, too, when you were all sleeping. Grabbed some of them rotten apples off the tree. Made me puke. Old Zack never knew." He spit in the water. "You a yellowbelly ?"

"No, just careful," Cody retorted.

Tucker stared at him. "You're real dark now aren't you? I heard old Zack ain't crazy about having a black kid for a grandson. Keeping you close to home ain't he, so no one will see you?"

Cody stared at him, knowing that Tucker's voice didn't carry to Zachariah. Should he dunk the creep or just get out and ignore him? It was one thing for Cody to think such things about his grandfather, entirely different for a stranger to say them.

"You just visiting here, right?" Tucker said, spurting a stream of water out of his mouth.

"Yes."

"Like one of them Fresh Air kids," Tucker said. "From the inner city."

"Wrong. From outer space! At night I turn into a Martian and zap smart-mouths." Cody hauled himself up on the dock. Talk about water pollution! Cody wouldn't put it past Tucker to pee in the pond either.

Tucker swam to the dock and slapped more water up at Cody. "Take that, you bag of crap!" Turning, he dove under, swimming as fast as he could for the other side.

Cody dove in. He sensed rather than saw the white legs churning ahead of him and with a burst of speed caught Tucker by one ankle, held him back as he counted to three, then let him go.

Cody surfaced a fraction of a second before Tucker. When he came up, Tucker had a look of terror on his face.

"You better not come sneaking over here to go swimming in the dark, anymore," Cody said. He pointed up to the windows in his back bedroom. "My bed's right there. I'll stay awake watching for you. And if I catch you..."

Zachariah who had been weeding a flower bed around the porch, straightened up as Tucker ran screeching down the driveway to the street.

"What's the matter with him?"

"That kid's a smart mouth. I got tired of it. So I held him under water for a couple of seconds. We were both under. I think I scared him."

Zachariah's mouth got that tight look that had disappeared in the last few days. "What'd he say?"

Cody shrugged. Tucker's name calling had been stupid and embarrassing. He didn't feel like repeating it. "Nothing important."

Zachariah's face grew dark. "I've got to keep on living here after you go home. His grandmother's not going to be happy."

Zachariah paused, his anger gathering steam. "Is that the kind of behavior your mother and stepfather teach you? What is it with your kind anyway? *You people think*

100

violence is the answer to everything?"

Cody shrunk as if Zachariah had hit him. He stared past him, his ears hot, the pain in his middle making him want to throw up. Swallowing, he forced himself to stand there, waited for another attack, but it didn't come.

Cody had been about to tell Zachariah that Tucker had been sneaking in here after dark, but he didn't. Serve them both right if Tucker drowned some night. Here was Zachariah taking some rotten kid's side against his grandson, his namesake.

It was clear to Cody that Alice Hubbard, and her relatives, were more important to Zachariah than his own flesh and blood.

"Well?"

Zachariah was waiting for him to say something, but there was no way Cody would say, "I'm sorry," because he wasn't. Tucker Hubbard had a dunking and more coming to him.

But it wasn't Tucker he hated. He wasn't worth it. Cody's mother said hate was love turned inside out. Now he knew it was true. Cody had wanted to love his grandfather. But how could you love someone who not only didn't love you back, but made it his business to let you know it?

He went inside, up to his bedroom, took off the wet cutoffs and found some dry clothes. Picking up the wet shorts, he heard voices in the backyard.

He could hear Zachariah calling him as he went down the stairs. Tucker was on the back porch with his father. Mr. Hubbard looked like Tucker only his belly stuck out, red and ugly, between his pants and shirt, while Tucker's caved in.

"This is Tucker's father," Zachariah said. "He says you threatened Tucker and tried to drown him."

Cody met Mr. Hubbard's gaze. "We were both under

water. I was just making a point. I don't like being called names."

Mr. Hubbard turned to Tucker. " Did you call him names?"

"No!" Tucker's smirk was gone.

Mr. Hubbard glanced from Zachariah to Cody. "These boys from the ghetto...don't always know how to act with civilized people."

Zachariah opened his mouth and hope leaped inside Cody that his grandfather would come to his defense. But nothing came out.

Cody would have to do it himself. "I don't live in a ghetto, but if I did, I'd still be civilized enough not to sneak into other people's ponds at night. I don't break branches off trees and throw apples all over either."

Zachariah stared at Tucker. So did his father.

"You've been coming over here swimming again at night?" Mr. Hubbard shouted. "You want to drown?" He didn't say anything about the apple trees, just took Tucker by the arm and walked him bellyaching out of the yard without apologizing to Zachariah for the broken branches.

It was hard to tell what his grandfather was thinking. Cody waited, knowing it was useless, for some word that Zachariah understood Cody just couldn't take the garbage the jerk had been dishing out. Maybe even an apology for the way he'd turned on Cody.

Instead, pale lips clamped together, his grandfather walked away without even glancing at him.

A cold shiver went through Cody, but it wasn't from the icy swim.

He started walking. It was time to call it quits. He'd had nothing but grief since he came to Turtle Rock and the hurt inside now was a twisting knife slicing him into little bits.

He'd been performing his own version of the Sun

102

Dance, torturing himself to prove he was worthy to be part of his father's family. And for what? So Zachariah could stand up for a lying, sneaking snake.

Without realizing where he was walking, Cody found himself headed up to the deer lick. He needed a quiet place to think, to decide what to tell his mother when he called her. He knew it was going to hurt her even worse than it did him that she had been right about Zachariah all along.

Chapter 14

Cody chose a cool spot under a tall pine from which he could see both the deer lick and the house.

His back against the bumpy trunk, he sat for a long time sorting things out, trying to make them come out the way he'd wanted them to. He knew now he'd come to Turtle Rock in part to prove his mother wrong about Zachariah. But there was no getting around the truth.

He started to the house, changed his mind and went to the barn instead for a look at his shelf. Running his fingers over the surface, he admired his work. It would be the only thing he had to show for his visit here. That and the railroad spike. The watch was gone.

He looked around the barn, knowing he'd never come back to Turtle Rock. Now he'd never see what the barn would look like when Zachariah turned it into a home, would never know if his grandfather had planned adding a room for him in the loft.

He took his time going to the house. Zachariah was sitting in the rocker, just looking out the window. It wasn't like his grandfather to sit around in the daytime. He looked tired and white under his sunburn. Had he taken his heart pill that morning? Cody couldn't remember.

He went upstairs to his father's room, pulled out the big suitcase and started packing his clothes. He'd wait until tonight when Zachariah had gone to bed to call his mother and ask her to come get him.

As he emptied the top drawer of socks, he glimpsed the postcard she'd sent. He'd forgotten. She was in Toronto. There was the phone number staring at him. But if he called her at the hotel, she'd panic. He'd just have to tough it out for another day or so.

Back downstairs Zachariah hadn't moved. "I'm going to ride around on the bike for a while," Cody told him.

"What?" His grandfather seemed to be in a fog.

"I'm going for a bike ride."

Zachariah didn't nod, didn't growl "be careful" the way he usually did.

It felt strange riding around without Jem. His first stop was the supermarket where he bought a can of pop and a couple of sticks of beef jerky. From there he rode to the lake.

The little park was empty and he rode to the swinging bridge, lay the bike down and crossed to the turtle rock, perching on it to drink his pop. He stuck the jerky in his jeans pocket and watched a wild duck and her babies swimming near the bank.

When they swam away he got up and wandered around, remembering when Jem had first brought him there. The rock still reminded him of a hamburger although if he stood in a certain spot and really used his imagination he could see the shape of a turtle shell and even a head emerging.

He felt restless and headed for home. When he got to the driveway, he heard his name and saw Jem waving at him from her front porch. He left the bike near the Christmas tree sign and went over.

"You're not sick?"

"Not anymore. It's so hot I thought we could go swimming in the pond, but Mom says I have to wait until tomorrow."

"I was in before and it's kind of cold." That approach seemed better than an outright apology. He didn't mention Tucker.

"Stay and eat with us, okay? Mom called Grandpa and he's just going to have a dish of cold greens because it's too hot to eat, but said you can stay if you want."

Cody was happy he didn't have to be in the house alone with Zachariah. He stayed at Jem's until bedtime, playing with the puppies until it got dark and then coming in to play a video game with her while the adults read the newspaper.

Jem walked out to the porch with him when he left. "Tomorrow we can go up and look for the watch, okay?"

"Maybe," he said to put her off. There was no use going up to Devil's Den. They'd never find the watch and even if they did, it would be ruined after all the rain.

"We'll have to go in the afternoon. I've got a checkup at the dentist at 11."

"Okay." At the house, Zachariah was dozing in the rocker as if he'd never moved. Cody tiptoed up the stairs, not wanting to wake him and then have to talk to him. He tossed and turned for a while remembering everything Zachariah had said to him since the first words at the airport. Thinking about it made him sick, sicker than he had been that first night.

The next morning he went up to the barn and worked

on the shelf for his mother. Zachariah and Cody grunted at each other when it was absolutely necessary and Cody avoided the smaller garden next to the house where his grandfather was hoeing.

At noon he took a swim while he waited for Jem to come back and was sunning himself on the dock when the phone rang. Zachariah was in the barn, so Cody tore off down the yard to answer it. Maybe his mother had come home early.

It was Steve Gustafson. "We're going up to Prospect to swim and camp overnight. Can you come?"

"What's Prospect?"

"A hill. There's a pond on top with a diving board."

"We've got a pond here," Cody said.

"It's more fun on Prospect. We're going to build a fire, roast hot dogs. Dad's on vacation this week and so we're doing something fun every day."

"I'll have to ask my grandfather," Cody said, not wanting to go, but not wanting to stay around the house either.

Zachariah merely nodded when Cody asked and he went up and repacked the gym bag with just a change of clothes, throwing the other things into the big suitcase. He was glad that his grandfather was acting that way. It made it easier in the long run. But Jem came before the Gustafsons did. She was bubbling over about how she just knew they'd find the watch when she spotted Cody's gym bag on the porch.

"Steve Gustafson called and asked me to camp out with them on Prospect."

Jem's face crumpled. "I thought finding the watch was important to you."

"It is but..." He stopped. How could he tell her that he couldn't stand being here? That being around family was too painful?

"You're still mad at me over losing the watch."

"No, I'm not. It's just that..."

"That you like the Gustafsons better! I thought you liked me as a friend, not just a cousin."

"I do. And I don't like the Gustafsons better."

"Then how come you treated me like I wasn't there all day at the dam and now after we made plans, you're going with them?"

Cody didn't get a chance to answer.

"Never mind. I've got better things to do than worry about a person you can't depend on." She glared at him. "And you are still mad about the watch! I can tell."

"And I can tell I need to spend some time with people who aren't babies," he lashed out. It was a mean thing to say and he was sorry as soon as he said it, but Jem was already running out of the yard.

The Gustafson pick-up pulled into the driveway. Steve and Kyle were in the back sandwiched in with the camping equipment. They yelled at him to get in.

"Go ahead, Cody, jump in." Mr. Gustafson got out of the cab. "I want to see your grandpa for a minute and see if he knows why I've got beautiful, big tomato plants, but no tomatoes."

Cody climbed onto the truck bed and squeezed down between Steve and Kyle who were wrangling over who got what sleeping bag. Mr. Gustafson was back in a minute.

"Too much fertilizer according to your grandpa." He winked at Cody and got into the driver's seat.

Kyle and Steve waved goodbye to Zachariah who stood in the barn doorway. He looked different from a distance--older and not so strong, Cody thought. Zachariah waved back, using the red scarf from his neck, his gaze moving to Cody. Cody half raised his hand, then quickly dropped it. He couldn't take much more of this...

The dirt road up to the top of Prospect was steep and winding, but Mr. Gustafson's pickup took the curves well. The top of the hill was grassy and open, far wider than the mountain top at Devil's Den.

Under their father's direction, Steve and Kyle put up a tent for sleeping and a canopy for cooking in case it rained while Cody finished unloading the truck. It was late afternoon by the time they got around to swimming in the pond. Having the hilltop to themselves, they stripped off their clothes and jumped in without trunks.

"Isn't this great having no girls around?" Kyle asked. Cody nodded without enthusiasm.

They had just started a fire to cook supper when they spotted dust clouds and a car coming up the hill. It was Mrs. Gustafson.

"The water heater broke and the basement's flooded," she announced. "Sorry, guys."

"We can stay by ourselves," Steve pleaded. "We're old enough and responsible. Nothing will happen."

But Mr. Gustafson refused to leave them on Prospect. Cody watched as the tents came down faster than they'd gone up.

"Rats!" Kyle was openly angry and Steve kicked up a cloud of dust around the doused fire.

"We'll try it again before Cody has to leave for the summer," their father promised.

Back in town he let Cody out in front of the farm-house and quickly speeded away. Cody heard someone calling him and turned to see Aunt Charlotte.

"Cody, I can't get anybody to answer the phone at Grandpa's. Will you tell Jem to come home? She's been there a long time. Timmy's still napping and I don't want to leave him."

Cody went around to the back where Zachariah was

just coming out of the barn. Without looking at his grand-father, Cody explained what had happened on Prospect and added, "Aunt Charlotte's looking for Jem."

"Must be in the house or did I see her head up to the deer lick?" Zachariah looked up at the overcast sky. "Could be a storm headed our way. Rainiest spell we've had in a while."

Cody started to say something, then thought he'd bet-ter not. He was pretty sure he knew where Jem was.

In the kitchen, he grabbed the sweatjacket he'd thrown on a chair and beef jerky sticks left from the day before.

Quickly he wrote a note to Zachariah telling him he was going to Devils Den to bring Jem home and stuck it on the refrigerator door.

And then hoping Zachariah didn't see him, he started up the hill. With luck, he'd get up to the logging road before the rain started. Once he found Jem, he'd make her run down the hill. She must be hunting for the watch and not aware of the time or that a storm was coming.

He went as fast as he could, slipping on damp leaves a couple of times in his eagerness to get to the road. Once he was on it, he could really move and if he went straight up, instead of curving over, it might save time in the long run.

He climbed steadily, only half noticing a squawking blue jay and two squirrels jumping from one tree to an-other. Halfway up he flushed out a pheasant which took off with a great flapping of wings. Cody jumped a foot. "All that bear talk is getting to me," he muttered.

The newspaper had said bears almost never hurt you, only if you were cutting off their exit or there were cubs around. Still he didn't think he wanted to meet up with one.

Out of breath, he reached the road in half the time it had taken before. At the big rock with the devil's head painted on it, he began calling Jem. No answer. He walked around and tried calling again. After a while, he began to give up hope.

If she hadn't come up here, where was she? The sky was black and he felt the first big drops of rain on his face. He started to untie the sweatshirt he had around his waist to put over his head before running down the hill when he heard a noise. It sounded like someone calling his name.

"Jem!" He yelled as loud as he could. "Where are you?"

No answer.

He tried again and again and was wondering if he had imagined it when he heard her.

"Cody!"

He yelled her name, but got no response. "Keep calling, Jem. Where are you?" Another call, this time fainter, came from up near the Flats. He ran in that direction and soon spotted her, her shirt and shorts bright against the gray rocks. She was leaning against one of them, standing on one foot. Relief flooded through him.

"Oh, Cody." Her face was covered with tears and streaks of mud. He ran to her and she threw her arms around him, giving him a quick hug before she collapsed on the ground. "I was afraid nobody would find me."

"Are you okay? What happened?" He eased down beside her.

"I came up to find the watch because I knew inside you were still mad at me. I heard a huge crashing noise and got scared. I started to run and twisted my ankle on one of the rocks. Scraped it too. I didn't have anything to stop the bleeding but my socks."

"Oh, Cody," she said, one tear sliding down her dirty face, "I found the watch. It's ruined."

She held the pocket watch out to him. He took it, his

heart sinking. He could barely see the numerals under the cloudy crystal.

"I don't think it will ever run again." More tears ran down Jem's dirty face. "Grandpa will be so mad at us," she wailed.

Cody half turned so she couldn't see his face and put the watch in his pocket.

"It doesn't matter," he said. Nothing mattered any more. "And I'm the one to blame. I brought it up here." He paused to emphasize his next words, "And I'm not mad at you, just at myself for acting like a nerd. Now let's get going." As he spoke, a clap of thunder sounded. Big rain drops splashed on their heads.

"I want to go home, but I don't know if I can make it."

"We'll have to hurry," he said. "Here lean on me this way."

Her ankle was giving her pain and he could see she was having trouble walking even on the level surface of the logging road. Jem might look light, but she was solid. If only he were bigger, he could carry her on his back. But it would be much worse going down the hill, dodging slippery leaves and holes.

A sudden crash of thunder made them both cringe.

"Jem," Cody said quietly, "we're going to have to wait here until the rain stops.He pointed toward the two big boulders that formed a cave, the one he had dubbed Cody's Castle.

"No! Cody, we can't stay here!" Jem shuddered. "I told you before that I heard something crashing through the woods. Whatever it was, it was humongous, Cody. It cut through down there, right below me. I couldn't see because of the trees. Oh, Cody, I know it was a bear!"

Chapter 15

"It couldn't have been a bear," Cody said. "Remember what your dad was telling us the other night about bears liking marshy places? This is the top of the mountain. And even if it was a bear, they don't bother people. Not if we don't bother them."

Jem got that stubborn look he'd learned to recognize. "It had to be a bear. Nothing else could make that much noise." Her voice rose. "And how could anybody be sure that a bear won't attack? It's an animal. A wild animal!"

Cody studied his shoe laces. He didn't want her to see she was making him nervous. "Even if it was a bear, it doesn't mean it will come back. And if it does, we'll crawl in the cave."

"And it'll crawl right in after us!"

"If we go way to the back, it couldn't see us." Cody tried to sound as if he knew what he was talking about. "You crawl in and I'll sit in front of you. If the bear comes--if there really is a bear--I'll jump out and start running and it'll chase me and you'll be safe."

"But you can't run fast, Cody," Jem argued. "I always beat you."

It was true. She always did beat him, even when he ran as fast as he could while pretending not to race.

He clenched his hands. "You got any better ideas?"

But Jem was already sliding over the dry, dead leaves and small branches to the back of the cave, moaning as her ankle scraped the ground.

"It stinks in here. What if this is a bear's bed?"

"They only hibernate in the winter."

"I'm getting wet. The rain's coming in the little air hole in the back," Jem complained.

"Take this." He undid the sweatshirt he'd tied around his waist and gave it to her. "Put it on."

"Now you're cold. I can see the goosebumps on your arms."

"No I'm not." The temperature had dropped, but the goosebumps were from fear, not the cold. What if she was right? He wasn't sure black bears wouldn't attack either. The reporter who'd written the newspaper story had probably never seen a bear.

The sprinkle had increased to a shower and was gusting in through the back. Jem crept closer to him. He could feel her warm breath on his back through the thin tee shirt.

If the rain didn't stop, they'd have to wait until morning to get down. They couldn't chance it in the dark, not with Jem hurt.

He felt a shudder go through her. It had grown dark, but he knew it had to be because of the storm and the deep leaf cover overhead. It really wasn't that late.

"Cody?"

"Umm?"

114

"Did you eat before you started up here? I'm hungry."

"I didn't take time, but I grabbed these." He reached into his pants pocket and came up with only one stick of beef jerky. The other must have fallen out.

"I had one on the way up," he lied. He'd eaten a few potato chips while they were building the fire on Prospect. That would have to hold him.

Jem peeled off the clear wrap and took a bite. "I didn't think I liked jerky, but when you're hungry it's not so bad. I looked for something to eat, but it's too late for strawberries and too early for blackberries."

As she munched away, Cody's stomach rumbled, but he ignored it. It was his fault Jem had come up here. Aunt Charlotte and Uncle Rob would be furious and Zachariah was already mad at him for dunking Tucker Hubbard. They'd all be glad when he went home early.

If only the thing with Tucker hadn't happened, he could have stayed, pretended that there wasn't a mile-wide split between him and his family. He had his dad's old room and was sleeping in his bed, living in the house his dad had grown up in.

Sometimes Cody imagined his dad bedded down in the bunk over him, the two of them in the warm darkness talking easy the way people do who've known each other forever. Once he'd felt--was sure--that Zack Jr. was there in the room, telling him to hang in there, that he understood what Cody was dealing with, telling him, without words, the one thing Cody most wanted to hear in the whole world.

He reached inside his pocket and curved his hand around the pocket watch. It would never run again, but it was something his dad had treasured, something Zack Jr. had touched and held.

His thoughts turned to J.B. His dad would have loved the pup, too. If Cody had stayed long enough, Zachariah might have softened and let him bring the pup in the house.

He stared at the dirt floor of the cave hating himself, hating Zachariah, hating the way everything had turned out. If only his grandfather had taken Cody's side instead of that weasel Tucker's. His stomach growled and this time Jem heard it. "Oh, Cody, you're hungry, too."

"It doesn't matter." He just hoped someone would come soon. Stupid that he hadn't told anyone where he was going. What if Zachariah or Aunt Charlotte never looked at the refrigerator door?

He had, Cody realized, changed his mind about the mountains. They didn't make him feel closed in as they had at first. They were more like sheltering walls. But being on top one, trapped in Devil's Den all night, was a scary possibility.

The rain was letting up, but it was still quite dark. Jem let out a scream.

"Cody, look!" Green eyes peered at them through the dimness. "It's the bear!"

He could feel the hair stand up on the back of his neck. His heart thumped loudly until he realized whatever it was, it was too low on the ground to be a bear.

"Probably a woodchuck or rabbit or something small," he said when he could speak.

"Oh, Cody, I wish we were home," Jem wailed. So did he but wishing wasn't going to do any good. For the umpteenth time he cussed himself out for not telling anybody where he was going.

He shifted position, trying to get comfortable. Sitting cramped in one spot was cutting off his circulation, making him even colder.

"Cody," Jem moaned, "I thought Dad would come by now. Are you sure you left a note?"

"I told you. On the refrigerator. They'll see it. I know

they will." He tried to think of something positive to say.

"Look, it's getting lighter out," he said trying to make his voice upbeat.

"But it won't stay light with night coming."

"We won't be here that long," he reassured her, wishing he could believe it himself. She moved her foot and groaned and he knew she was crying. He felt like crying, too, but not for the same reason.

I'm sorry for acting like a baby." She sniffed. "But, I'm scared, Cody. If I could run, it would be different. But, if the bear comes, there's nothing I can do." She sniffed again. "I'm glad you're with me anyway. If you hadn't come I don't know what I'd have done."

"You'd have been okay. You're smart and you'd have kept your head, Jem." If he had to be stuck with any girl in a scary situation he was glad it was Jem. She was okay about other things too. She learned fast what bothered people and what didn't.

Jelly Belly had tried to tell Cody that white people, even white people who were relatives, were different than black people. That he would be unhappy in Turtle Rock. Jelly Belly had been half right.

Jem and Aunt Charlotte and Uncle Rob, and even little Timmy, had been real family. Then there was Zachariah. Tucker had been the worst, but Zachariah's words and the way he had acted had hurt more.

And Cody didn't want to stay around anybody who didn't care what hurt other people or made no effort to change. He'd stayed as long as he did because he, Cody Spain, was stubborn. Just like Zachariah. He hadn't wanted his grandfather to have the satisfaction of driving him away.

A picture of Zachariah rocking Timmy and singing "Froggie" suddenly came to mind. Funny he should think of that just now.

"Listen!" Jem got up on her knees leaning over his shoulder. "Do you hear that? It sounds like a car or voices." Cody leaned toward the mouth of the cave, heard branches soughing in the wind.

"No, I don't think so. "He listened again, heard nothing. And then suddenly a sound, this time very real, broke the silence.

Something was crashing through the underbrush. He turned to Jem to see if she'd heard it too. Her eyes grew large as she listened.

"It's the bear! I know it's the bear," she screamed.

"Shhh!" He listened again, heard nothing. The crashing sound was coming closer. Whatever it was, it was BIG! His heart felt as if it were in his throat. Why had he ever thought he wanted to see a bear up close?

"If it doesn't know we're here, it won't bother us," he repeated, knowing he didn't believe it any longer.

Miraculously the noise grew fainter. Whatever was making the crashing sound was moving away from them. At least he hoped it was.

"It's leaving, isn't it?" Jem whispered. He nodded, relief draining him as the noise faded away. Still he couldn't relax. How could anybody relax in a situation like this?

It was getting colder on top of the mountain. He crossed his arms over his chest and rubbed them to get his blood going. But when Jem tried to give him back his sweatjacket he refused. It was quiet then, so quiet he could hear himself breathing.

"Mom was going to barbecue chicken tonight," Jem said after a while.

"Don't," groaned Cody, but he was no longer hungry. Fear was all he felt. He couldn't unbend until they were out of this place. And that might not be until morning.

The whole mountain top seemed to be sleeping. No birds chirping, no squirrels chattering this time of night. Far different than the way it had been in the middle of the afternoon when they had watched the deer grazing in the sunlight.

Jem gasped. "Did you hear that?"

Cody lifted his head. A noise was ringing through the woods. There was no mistaking the sound of branches snapping under enormous weight.

"It's the bear coming back!" Jem yelled. Quickly he turned and put his hand over her mouth.

"You want it to hear us?"

Jem pushed his hand away. "Cody, I'm scared! Bears can run 30 miles an hour. It sounds like that now."

He had to admit, whatever it was, it was coming fast, getting closer. Jem's breathing was ragged. Suddenly she threw her arms around his neck strangling him from behind. "Cody! Do something! It's coming!"

As he watched, paralyzed, the huge animal came into view on all fours. It had to be a male, weighing hundreds of pounds. Cody gulped in air, his chest hurting, then forgot to breathe out as the bear suddenly stopped 20 yards below the cave near an old dying tree.

As they watched, it reared up on both back legs. Like a man with an itchy back, it rubbed up against the tree back and forth, removing dried mud. It was also a way bears left messages, Uncle Rob had said. Cody shrank. It was tall as Uncle Rob, at least.

Cody eyed its claws. They were mammoth. He shuddered and tried to think of a prayer, but he was too scared.

It was Jem's dry sobs and her whole body shaking that finally cut through his daze. He turned to her.

"If it comes this way, I'll start running. You...You get down on your stomach with your hands over your head."

"Cody! You can't! You're not fast enough."

"I don't think the bear will come here. We're above him and he can't smell us." He didn't know which was trembling worse, his voice or his legs. He was primed, ready to go, when the huge animal went back down on all fours again. It glanced up at the cave, sniffed the air once or twice, then looked their way. It took a couple of steps.

"It's coming right for us!" screamed Jem.

"Get down!" It was hard to make his voice work with his heart in his throat. For a second, he crouched at the mouth of the cave, glancing from the bear to the logging road just below. He would head for the road. It would be easier to run on the packed-down surface.

Then yelling as loud as he could to get the bear's attention, he tore down the slope. Blind with fear, he flew, stumbling once over a large tree root, righting himself, still yelling. He hit the road, saw a bend ahead, and looked back to see if the bear was coming.

It wasn't! That meant it was going to the cave.

"Jem!" he roared over his shoulder and slammed full force into something big and solid.

His scream tore at his throat, the sound ringing in his ears.

The bear had circled around and come back to tear him apart. He closed his eyes waiting for the first strike of the enormous claws.

Chapter 16

For a second he lost consciousness, his head lolling backwards. The bear was shaking him and growling his name. "Cody! Cody!"

He opened his eyes and slumped against his grandfather's chest, "Jem?" he moaned, and remembering, straightened up. "The bear! Jem?"

"Jem's all right. Her daddy's got her. As for the bear, you scared the living daylights out of that critter." Zachariah loosened his hold for a second and looked down into Cody's face, then pulled him back tightly against his chest. One big hand cradled his head, the other moved up and down his back. Cody couldn't remember anything ever feeling so good.

"Cody!" It was Jem, held high in Uncle Rob's arms who finally turned him around. "You okay?"

He nodded, still trying to take everything in, not able to talk. He saw his grandfather take off his jacket and felt the wooly warmth encircle him.

Zachariah began guiding Cody down the logging road toward the Blazer. He could hear Jem chattering a mile a minute telling Uncle Rob everything that had happened.

He heard his name again and again. "A hero just like Uncle Zack," she said.

Cody shook his head. He wasn't. He'd never been so afraid in his life. Though from what they were saying, it sounded as if the bear had been even more afraid, running off at the first sound of Cody's voice.

It was a long walk to the Blazer. A tree had gone down in a previous storm across the road, blocking its way.

When they reached it, Cody and Zachariah piled into the back while Uncle Rob settled Jem in the front. She was still chattering away, telling about finding the watch and how she'd fallen when she first heard the bear.

In spite of Zachariah's jacket, a shiver went through Cody and his grandfather unexpectedly put an arm around him, pulling Cody to him. Cody sucked in air. He wasn't dead, because Zachariah's warmth was flowing through his body. He wasn't dreaming either. This, he thought, was how Timmy must feel when Zachariah rocked him -- safe and...

Cody put his hand in his pocket and cradled the watch. After a moment, he pulled it out, holding it up so his grandfather could see it. "Jem found the watch. My fault it's ruined," he said.

Zachariah ignored the watch, barely visible in the increasing darkness. "I found your bags packed when we were looking for you two. You going home?"

"I have to," Cody said.

His grandfather's arm tightened around Cody. They backed down the rutted logging road, then at a point where the road forked, the Blazer was turned around.

Uncle Rob had turned on the heater and it was making Cody drowsy. He dozed off for a moment, then roused aware that Zachariah's arm was still around him. Maybe he was dreaming.

"I thought you hated me," he mumbled.

"*Hated you?*" Zachariah leaned closer to catch his words.

"Me and my mother...for...for...being different, for being black."

"Is that why you are going?"

Cody nodded. "I started to call my mother to come get me, but she's in Toronto. She won't be home until tomorrow."

For a long time there was only the sound of the Blazer's tires on the dirt road. When Zachariah spoke his voice was tired and old-sounding and Cody had to strain to hear.

"I don't hate you. And I don't hate your mother, though I can see why she'd think so.

"I made a mistake a long time ago--when your daddy said they were getting married. I thought they were asking for trouble."

"You mean people would give them a hard time?"

"And their children. You." There was a long pause. "Your Grandma Gemma...said it wasn't our place to get in the middle of it. She said parents had to support their kids' decision."

"Grandma Gemma didn't mind about my mom and dad getting married?"

"She worried for the same reasons I did, but she liked your mama from the start. Said Vanessa had a good heart and good upbringing and that was all that mattered."

"But you didn't think so?"

"I knew Gemma was right." There was another long pause. "But still I tried talking sense to your daddy and when he wouldn't budge, wouldn't listen to a word I said, I blamed your mother."

Cody tried to interrupt, but Zachariah went on.

"A man can be afraid of something that's different from what he's used to. When I looked at your mother, I wasn't seeing her, I was seeing something foreign, almost scary like those CCC fellows.

"Another thing--I wasn't used to having my faults pointed out, but your mother didn't hold back. I got hot under the collar."

Zachariah didn't wait for Cody to answer. "When your daddy died, it broke our hearts. I tried to get your mother to come here and raise you. I thought I could make up for the grief I caused her and Zack Jr. And, of course, we wanted Zack's boy here near us. You were all we had left of him. But when I asked Vanessa, it came out the wrong way. Things have been bad between us ever since."

All was quiet in the back seat, the sound of the Blazer tires signaling they were off the mountain road, on paved surface.

Zachariah was mumbling and Cody could barely hear him.

"I'd give the rest of my life to take back all the things I said--for things to be better between us. Don't you know, boy...? Don't you know...?" His grandfather's voice broke... "I love you, Cody boy."

He must be dead! The bear had got him after all. This couldn't be his grandfather talking. Not Zachariah! Cody groped for words, but nothing came out.

"Looks like you've made up your mind. You'll be calling your mother, I suppose?" Zachariah's voice slid off into the darkness.

Cody was quiet, thinking of the dream. At the deer lick, Zack Jr. had told Zachariah the train had left. But trains could slow down, could back up, could let a late passenger hop on. Still there was something that bothered him...

"But when I finally came, you were still mad at me. All you did was growl, say mean things..."

"Yes, I suppose I did...Thought I'd die from joy at the airport. I couldn't believe that you were actually here. My dead boy's son! There's so much of him in you. I was scared, too, and with good reason. You said right off you might not be staying long."

Zachariah took a deep breath. "I knew I had to steel myself against caring too much. I figured we didn't mean much to you. Then that first night at Charlotte's you told us about your stepfather wanting to adopt you--about changing your name..."

"*But I'm not! I couldn't,*" Cody cried. "It's my dad's name, your name." The words came tumbling out before he could pull them back. "I love you, too, Grandpa... all of my dad's family..."

Zachariah let out a strangled sound and gathered Cody to him, cutting off his words. For a minute Cody was worried about his grandfather's heart. But when he spoke Zachariah's voice was steady, firm.

"Thank the Lord!" He took another deep breath. "About Tucker...He won't be coming over any more. I talked to his grandmother."

"About the apples?"

"About the name-calling. I knew you didn't lie--that you had been brought up right. Your mother's done a good job raising you." Zachariah looked out the window though it was too dark to see anything. "You can tell her I said so."

Cody dozed off then, breathing in the scent of his grandfather's jacket, a faint mixture of wet wool, wood shavings and prize manure. He woke as they pulled in the driveway of the farmhouse, Zachariah's arm still around him.

It was night now and the kitchen was a warm glow in the darkness, light streaming from the big windows.

As the Blazer came to a stop, the kitchen door was flung open and Aunt Charlotte came running out, followed by Max carrying Timmy.

"Oh, God," he heard his aunt say. He couldn't tell if she was crying or laughing.

Zachariah waited until Uncle Rob lifted Jem from the Blazer, then pushed the seat forward and crawled out. Turning, he reached back to guide a sleepy Cody over the floor hump and around the tilted front seat.

"Cody come too?" Timmy's thin baby voice filled the still night.

A rush of warmth went through Cody. " Right here, Timmy!" he called back and, with one hand on his grandfather's arm, he jumped to the ground.

Chapter 17

In the warm, bright kitchen, there was so much noise and confusion, Cody's head was spinning. Aunt Charlotte and Max must have hugged him a dozen times as Jem gave an account of the whole night, repeating how Cody had saved her from being clawed to death.

He was embarrassed by all the attention and turned toward the table. Max baked in times of trouble. There was another of her pies, still steaming, the apple cinnamon scent filling the room.

"That sure smells good," he said. "I'm really hungry. Jem is too."

This set off more cries as Max went to the cupboard to get plates and glasses while Aunt Charlotte turned on the heat under the leftover barbecue. She was pulling a half gallon of milk from the refrigerator when she stopped in mid-motion.

"Oh, no! I almost forgot! Your mother called, Cody.

Wouldn't you know, tonight of all nights! I didn't want to upset her. Told her you were up on the hill with Uncle Rob and Grandpa. But, she could tell something was wrong. Call her right away. Here's the number at the hotel. She'll be waiting!"

"Everything okay?" He took the slip of paper Aunt Charlotte handed him.

"Just missing her boy."

"I'll call now," he said and headed for the living room, eager to tell his mother he'd be staying for the summer. He smiled at his grandfather who was rocking a sleepy Tim.

There was no answering smile. Instead the familiar hardness flashed across Zachariah's face, then was gone.

The old resentment rose anew, evaporating even as Cody turned the corner. It was going to take a while for his grandfather to change. Maybe he'd never completely accept Cody's mother despite his words in the Blazer.

But Cody was through walking a tightrope. He was who he was. It was up to his family, both sides, to accept it.

His stomach began growling as the smell of barbecue drifted in from the kitchen. Quickly, he reached for the phone.

THE END

Also by

Patricia Costa Viglucci

Cassandra Robbins, Esq.

A New York Public Library *Books for the Teenage* selection, 1988; A *Celebrating the Dream* selection, 1990.

"... *the novel has strongly nonracist and nonsexist messages...sensitive issues are explored with candor...This will grab romance readers and may make them think a little, too.*"

-- ALA Booklist.

"*Lively, witty...well-written...*"

-- Publisher's Weekly

"*Enjoyable...well-written...Addresses black issues honestly and positively...*"

-- BAYA (San Franciso Bay Area Librarians)

SUN DANCE AT TURTLE ROCK may be ordered by writing to Stone Pine Books, Patri Publications, P.O. Box 25184, Rochester, NY 14625.

Price is $4.95 plus $1.95 for shipping and handling. Discount for five or more books. (N.Y. residents add 8% sales tax.) Write to Stone Pine Books, Patri Publications, P.O. Box 25184, Rochester, NY 14625.

For Information about *CASSANDRA ROBBINS, ESQ*. write to the author in care of Stone Pine Books, Patri Publications, Box 25184, Rochester, NY., 14625.